Amo Jones

Intricate Love

Sinful Souls MC Book Two

Amo Jones

This book is a work of fiction. Any references to real events, real people, and real places are used fictitiously. Other names, characters, places and incidents are products of the Author's imagination and any resemblance to persons, living or dead, actual events, organisations or places is entirely coincidental.

Formatting by Swish Design & Editing
Editing by Swish Design & Editing
Cover design by Amo Jones
Cover image Bigstock Photo

ISBN-13: 978-1517730765
ISBN-10: 1517730767

Note: This story is not suitable for persons under the age of 18 or those who do not enjoy sexy, twisted relationships. This is a roller coaster, not a carousel.

*If the word "fuck" offends you, please don't read this book.

Welcome to the twisted world of Vicky Abrahams and Blake Rendon.

To my loving partner who has to put up with my smart arse mouth for the rest of his life.

I love you.

ACKNOWLEDGMENTS

Simon—My partner in crime, the Clyde to my Bonnie, and the love of my life. I could not have done all of this without your undying support. You have been the truth to my words and my number one critic. I love you so much, and I cherish the moments you have had to (at times) take up both roles, as mother and father while I locked myself up in my writing cave. I love you - *always and forever*.

My four little people—My four little critters who are the light of my life. They have tolerated (at times) a moody mother when all I wanted to do was write, but they enjoy all my guilt gifts and privileges once I'm finished a book, though. So it's a win-win.

Isis Te Tuhi—Thank you for always being the ear to my troubles, for going through the emotional rollercoasters of all these stories with me, you are my caramel soul sister. *The one and only, Mrs. R.F.*

Kaylene Osborn— I'm not sure where to start with this incredible woman. You are not just my editor, you're my friend. Thank you for always being there, and I love that I can share anything with you. You have made me smile on the days that I didn't really feel like smiling and you have kicked my arse in line when it was needed. I'm not sure where I'd be without you.

Addison Jane— Jeepers, my girl. Where have you been all my life? Thank you for all the support you have given me on my writing journey. You are amazing and I thank you every day for everything that you have shared with me. #kiwiauthorsunite (Kay, leave the hashtag alone. It is okay.)

My Readers—My beautiful readers, I love you all. Keep reading and keep writing those reviews. Each of you has contributed to me pushing through my rough patches. You make it all worth it, each and every one of you.

The Bloggers—Thank you to all the lovely bloggers who have been there from day one, and the new ones who have just started reading my stories now and sharing your honest reviews. You are all amazing and I thank you for taking the time out of your busy lives to read my book. I hold the utmost respect for you.

Lastly, thank you to all who have had to endure my yapping as I got excited about a plot in one of my books and all I wanted to do was talk about it. I know I talked your ears off, *so thank you*.

INTRICATE
LOVE
Sinful Souls
MC Book 2

PROLOGUE

VICKY

Fifteen Months Later

My eyes open, then close.

"Blake?" I attempt to scream, but my voice is not coming out. I can't see, everything is black. Why can't I see? "*Blake!*" My voice begins to get louder and I'm starting to panic.

What's happened?

Why can't I see anything?

Where am I?

Where is Pipper?

Oh my God, Pipper.

I try to move my fingers, but nothing is moving.

Am I dead?

My thoughts are jumbled. I drift deeper and deeper into the darkness of the unknown.

VICKY

Present Day

You know how they say the best relationships come from those who were friends first? Well, they lied.

"Vicky?" Jesse shakes me while trying to wake me after going three rounds of hard sex. "Vicky, I know you don't fall asleep that fast."

If we weren't friends before this, he wouldn't know that kind of information.

"What Jesse? I'm tired."

He rolls over, pulling his pants back on. "Yeah, you've said that every time for the whole five months we've been doing this."

That's me, going back and repeating the same mistake numerous times because apparently I never learn. Also, Jesse has the biggest dick I've ever seen in all my twenty-three years so that definitely plays a factor in my constant mistakes.

"Well then, you should be used to it. God Jesse! I'm not doing this with you tonight."

He pulls his hoodie on, before walking out of my bedroom for the last time ever.

I hate mornings, anyone that's even close to being happy in the mornings should be killed in their sleep. I'm dragging my sorry ass out of bed moping until I remember it's officially day one of spring break.

Fuck yes! I think as I pump my fist into the air. Despite the fact that I'm not going to see Alaina for a while, I'm happy to get the hell out of *Dodge*. A certain basketball player may have played a major part in my decision. I'm drinking coffee when Alaina walks in, with her beautiful blonde hair messy and all over the place.

I laugh. "You know you could totally be in a hair commercial, you have *that* much hair."

"Tell me about it," she replies, sipping her black drink of goodness.

"When are you leaving?"

"In about an hour or so."

"I'm going to miss your crazy ass. Keep in contact, okay?" she asks.

"I promise."

After saying my goodbyes to Alaina, I start packing my bags into my Black Mercedes CL convertible. Managing to squash everything in, I mentally prepare myself for a wild summer with one of my best friends Kalie. Pulling onto the main highway, I set off to my parents' beach house in Coronado.

After three hours of singing along to some of the best songs in history, I pull into the driveway of our large, over the top mansion. Turning my car off, I roll my eyes—my mother has the most extravagant taste and barely spends any time here.

Greta comes out to greet me; she still looks the same. My parents keep her on to maintain the house while we're not living here.

"Hello, Vicky. Can I help you with your bags? I've stocked up the fridge and freshened up the place for you, dear."

I hug her in appreciation. "Thanks, Greta. Girl, have you lost weight? You're looking good mama. Mr. Daniels must love tapping that ass!" She blushes while waving my comment away.

"Oh Vicky, stop!" She laughs while picking up a couple of my bags and carrying them inside. I follow her, making my way up the front steps and inside the house, straight into my bedroom. After unpacking everything into my drawers, I pick up my phone and send a text to Kalie. Kalie and I have been friends since we were little. We had planned to do the whole summer vacation together because her parents own a spot three houses down from me.

> Me: *Are you almost ready? I can come over in ten.*
> Kalie: *Ready when you are. ;)*

Making my way to her front door, she swings it open before I can knock.

"Vicky!" she squeals.

"Hey babe, how have you been?"

She looks back to me through her bright emerald green eyes. "I've been better, but let's go and get a drink." Kalie is stunning. When we were little, I always asked my mom why I didn't get her amazing green eyes. "Let's walk down, it's not very far."

The main beach is only a ten-minute walk from our house. We talk and laugh, catching up on old times while making our way into town.

Walking into the local bar that sits on the beach side—it's all palm trees and mojitos—I look around and notice there's not many people in here, except for a large group of big bikers that are sitting in the corner. I look over to them for a second before moving along, finding it strange that they're all good looking, every single one of them. I laugh to myself because they mustn't be *real* bikers. There's no way *real* bikers look like that.

"So," I say, dropping down onto the barstool. "Why so glum?"

She tucks her light brown hair behind her ear. "I ended things with my ex, and he didn't take it too kindly."

I reply between sipping on my drink, "Oh well, let's find some new toys for you to play with."

Kalie blushes a little, her cheeks turning a brighter shade of pink. I'd almost forget how innocent she is.

"What? Are you going to tell me he left you because you're a virgin?" I laugh at my ridiculous thought. When I look over at her, she drops her eyes down to her fingers. "Oh shit, no way!"

She nods her head. "I know it's hard to believe because I'm twenty-one. Who's twenty-one and still a virgin?" she scoffs embarrassingly. I down my drink, eager to get this show on the road.

"You mean who's twenty-one, still a virgin, and looks like you do? Yeah, I think you're on your own with that one."

I can't believe it; the girl must get harassed daily. All our talking has made me lose count of how many drinks we've had. I notice Kalie has really opened up and is coming out of her shell the more we chat.

"Oh God! Please don't tell me this is your first time drinking?" I scoff to myself because really, there's no way girls like this still exist.

She giggles. "Well, I've tried drinking before. But yes, this is the first time I've been...what's the term...buzzed?" She's laughing like it's the funniest joke she's ever heard.

My face drops. "Oh fuck!"

She places both hands on my shoulders before slurring, "It's fine Vicky, it's spring break!" she says wringing her hands in the air.

I am going straight to hell, with no passing go. However, she's right. Fuck it!

"Let's dance." Dragging her up onto the dance floor, where Drowning Pool's *'Bodies'* is playing loudly through the speakers. We're laughing and dancing when I gaze over to the bikers in the corner. I'd forgotten all about them. One, in particular, has had his eyes glued on me with a hungry stare on his face. He's sitting with his legs spread out, cocking his head sideways and a smirk playing on his lips. Taking one more pull of his drink, he gets up and makes his way toward me. "Oh shit," I mumble to myself. *There's no way I'm fit for a biker…*I think. Once he reaches me, he latches on to my hand, pulling me into him.

"You usually drink nine shots of tequila, four rum and cokes, and a beer at four o'clock in the afternoon?" he asks.

I smile up at him. "I find it incredibly scary that you've been counting my drinks if you weren't so undeniably good-looking." I see my drunken mind is doing all the talking for me. "What's your name, biker man?" I ask and he laughs.

"Biker man?" I nod my head. "Blake, what's yours?" I tilt my head to the side, trying to re-focus my eyes by blinking them.

"You're *so* tall. How tall are you exactly?" I almost stumble backward, until he catches me and laughs then replies, "Six-foot-two."

"I'm Vicky, this is Kalie." Kalie is dancing off in her own little world, probably not realizing the attention on her. I see Blake check her out, before smiling and looking back to me. Anyone with a clear set of eyes will tell you how stunning she is.

"Want to come sit?" he asks, nudging his eyes back toward his table.

"Are you a murderer?" I ask.

He pauses. "What?"

"I said, are you a murderer?" I repeat myself and he laughs a devilish laugh.

"Not today, I'm not."

I shrug. "I'll settle for that."

He shakes his head as we follow him back to his table. Taking in his appearance while he's not looking, he has dark blond hair standing messily around his head and it's a little on the short side. His eyes are dark brown, almost black and he has a natural golden tan.

He's almost to die for.

Almost.

BLAKE

Three Weeks Ago

"*Blake!* In here now," I heard Zane yell out from his office. I dragged Britney with me under my arm as I walked in.

"What can I do for you, boss?" He chuckled his evil as fuck laugh at me, which only ever meant one thing. *Fucking great.*

"Well, it's funny you ask that question," he replied as he sat forward, putting his joint out in the ashtray. "Something just came up."

I pushed Britney back out the door before I replied, "Go on…"

He laughed again, pushing back on his seat with a scrape. "Do you remember Joseph Vance? He was best friends with our fathers?" I sat back in my chair, getting ready to listen to another story I never been told.

"I've heard of him, yes." Anyone that hadn't heard of Joseph Vance had either been living under a rock or in an upper-class lifestyle. The man was notorious. If this had anything to do with him, I knew I had no choice in the decision.

"He needs us to watch over his daughter. So we need an easy transition into her life." I scratched my chin deep in thought, I already knew what he wanted me to do.

"You want me to get with her?"

"Did I say that? No. I want you with her best friend Vicky. Slide us into her life smoothly," he said with his mouth set in a hard line.

"You mean to tell me you're pimping me out?" I asked him as I took another hit of the best green I'd ever had.

"No, the girl is fucking hot. It's not that bad, I've seen you with worse," he said while smirking. I knew he was implying Brittany. The girl was just a good time.

"You're hilarious, fuckface. What's the plan?"

After we'd gone over the plan that was about to set me up with a future crazy ex-girlfriend no doubt, I agreed.

"Do you have any photos of her?" I asked.

"She's going to be at her parents' beach house in Coronado during the summer. We have to head down to set it all up."

Great! A future, crazy, spoiled, ex-girlfriend.

I groaned into my hands. "Why me, bro. Fuck."

He laughed. "Because it'll put your mouth to work. Here are her pictures."

Snatching them out of his hands, I looked down and saw a tall, leggy brunette. She looked fucking hard to get, and uptight to match.

"*Fucking perfect,*" I said to myself sarcastically. "Fine, let's get this shit rolling then."

Three weeks later

We pull up to the hotel that we're all staying at and I look over at Zane.

"This is messed up and you know it."

He laughs while throwing his helmet onto his bike. "Oh, I know it."

We sign in and make our way to our rooms, nothing special but they'll do.

"She's making her way toward a bar downtown. Let's go," Zane murmurs as he's hanging up his phone. Here we go, the bitch is going to be stuck up as hell and worth way more trouble than any pussy is worth.

Pulling into the bar and making our way inside, we grab a seat and get ready for the most pathetic performance I'm ever going to have to give. I *do not* date girls. I've never done the girlfriend thing, and I'm never going to be interested in doing the girlfriend thing. Girls are too much trouble. *Just do the deed and be gone*. I order a beer while we wait.

"At least she's hot, bro. Pucker up those lips," Ade says, laughing between drinks.

I narrow my eyes at him. "Fuck up, Ade. You just wait."

It's not long before we see her making her way into the bar. She looks way fucking hotter in real life than in those pictures. Those damn legs, they go on forever. Her long brunette hair falls down her back. And that tight little body, has my dick twitching in my pants.

"Holy fuck," Harvey whispers as they walk past. "Oh, come on. I could've done it Z, and I would've appreciated that pussy too!" We all burst out laughing, typical fucking Harvey. Looking over at

Ade I notice he hasn't said anything since they walked in. That's just not like Ade to not say anything at all. I find his eyes glued on the hottie standing with Vicky. I bring my bottle back to my lips and internally laugh while looking at him. He notices and swings his head around to me, playing with a toothpick in his mouth.

"What?" he snaps.

"Oh, nothing brother. You might want to wipe that bit of drool off your chin, though." I take a swipe at his chin before he slaps my hand away with a smirk.

"Got jokes, huh? You just go make a girl crazy."

I'm still smirking when I look up to examine her, waiting for my opportunity and counting her drinks in the process. *The girl can put them away.* They begin to make their way to the dance floor, in the prime state for any rapist or modern day creep to walk up and take advantage of their situation. I see Vicky turn around, dancing her sexy as fuck body around in the air on the dance floor. Her eyes meet mine, and she holds my stare for what feels like hours before smiling and looking away. *That is my cue.*

So I take another drink of my beer and start making my way over to her.

VICKY

Sitting down at the table, I look over to Kalie and see her glancing every two seconds to one of the guys at the table, who's absolutely covered in tattoos and has a ring in his nose.

Shit, he's scorching hot.

The way she's eye fucking him right now, I know she's called dibs on him.

You snooze, you lose.

Blake does the introductions and I actually cannot believe how good looking these men are.

"Are you guys serious?" I ask. "I don't even see this many good looking guys in one whole day, as I have sitting here right in front of me." They laugh while Zane, I think his name is, pulls out a chair for me.

"Thanks, darling, take a seat."

There's no foreplay needed with this bunch, and I think quietly to myself that I'd totally have a go at taking them all in one sitting.

Don't judge me.

I point over to my very drunk friend. "This is Kalie." They all tilt their heads to her in *that* way guys usually do to greet each other. I notice the hottie in the corner still hasn't taken his eyes off her. He's smirking around the toothpick in his mouth.

Good luck with this one, friend.

We're all sipping on our drinks and talking when Blake leans into my ear and whispers, "Wanna get out of here?" I laugh then take another drink.

"Is that your way of asking to have sex with me?" I flutter my eyes at him, and he chuckles.

"I don't need to ask. You'll be begging me to put my dick in you once I'm done." I almost spit out my drink, so I quickly cover my mouth with my hand before laughing. "Talk is cheap, homeboy."

He pulls my seat over to him, picking me up and putting me on his knee. I look down at him, and for a brief second I feel like my heart may have stopped. I know it's only because he has me feeling *that* horny with next to no effort at all. Now my whole body is alert at his presence.

He tucks my hair behind my ear, putting his hand around the back of my neck, and pulls me down to his lips. At first, I try to fight his soft teasing kisses, but then he smiles against my lips, setting me off. I softly, slowly, pull at his bottom lip with my teeth, smiling when I hear his breath catch with a hiss escaping his mouth.

"Yeah, let's go," he mumbles seriously, picking me up and placing me back on the floor.

I look over to Kalie. "Wait, I can't go without Kalie."

He looks over to her sitting to my right, and then looks back to me. "Bring her."

I look at him, eyes wide. "I'm sorry, what?"

He smirks, with massive amounts of mischief playing in his eyes. "You heard me, bring her."

Looking to Kalie before sitting back down next to her, I whisper in her ear, "Do you want to come?"

She looks at me, her eyes as big as marbles. "Where?"

Blake brings his face between ours and whispers, "On Vicky's face."

I roll my eyes up at him then look back at Kalie, who is looking at Ade—he doesn't realize, though, not with a half-naked girl spread wide across his lap. My face scrunches up in disgust.

She looks back at me before looking up at Blake. "Okay."

We stand from the table and Blake throws his arms around both Kalie and me. "We out, I'll take the truck."

I look over at Ade, who's still not come up for air from the face he's currently sucking. *Oh well, his loss.* I am not bisexual, but I am all for experimenting this summer, so why not? Besides, Kalie is out of this freaking world gorgeous.

I hear Harvey yell in agony, "Oh come on! This shit is *not* fair." Zane looks up to me and winks.

God, can I have him too?

Walking out of the bar, I look over to Blake. "You know, if I do this you owe me, right?"

He laughs. "Owe you? My dick is your reward, and trust me he doesn't disappoint." I fake laugh as we get into the truck.

"No, I mean you owe me, and I want Zane."

He stops laughing and looks at me. "You what?" he asks with a smirk on his face that says, *'I'm in this for a good time, not a long time'* which works perfectly for me.

"You'll owe me for doing this, and I want Zane in my biker sandwich," I reply, wiggling my eyebrows.

He chuckles. "As hot as fuck as you are, I've never known him to be down like that. I might have someone in mind, though."

"If it's any of those sexy beasts sitting on that table, I'm down," I say while sliding into his car.

He laughs again while pulling out of the bar car park. "All right homegirl. Deal?"

Walking up to the room, I pull on Kalie to double check that she's still keen on this and to know her boundaries.

"K? Are you sure you want to do this?"

She looks at me with a smile. "I know what you're thinking, but yes I'm sure. No sex, though, I still want my V-card when I walk out."

I nod my head in understanding. Blake swings open the door, so we make our way inside while he pours drinks. This is extremely awkward, and I have no idea how this is supposed to begin, but it seems Blake does. He walks back to the living room area with drinks in his hand. I look around and it's quite a nice hotel actually, for what I was thinking anyway.

"Don't tell me you guys are all rich too?" I ask with sarcasm laced in my tone.

He looks over at me and winks "You'll never know."

He steps up to Kalie, and I see her looking at him with hunger in her eyes. It is hard not to, Blake is one sexy fine man, and he is *all* man. His body towers over her, and I watch as they have a moment.

Don't be a pussy, Vick. Do not pull that jealous shit.

Kalie lifts her hands up, running them over the front of his cut and wrapping her hand around his neck. He stops her by taking hold of her hands and bringing them back down right before his lips smash down to meet hers. Their kiss is hot, *holy fuck is it hot.* It's as if live porn is playing out right in front of me, with the two hottest leads you could ever think of. Kalie moans into his mouth, he picks her up wrapping her legs around his waist before throwing her onto the bed. He looks over to me, still sitting on the end of the bed. His eyes looking darker than I remember, his lips pouty and a smudge of red is shining on his cheek. He begins to walk to me, so I quickly down my drink in one huge gulp. Hooking his finger under my chin, he lifts my head before laying a sweet kiss on my lips.

Hold the fuck up.

"Wait, how come she gets that hot kiss, but all I get is a peck?"

He chuckles, pulling me back into his arms and whispering against my lips so only I can hear, "Trust me when I say this. I want to ravage more than your mouth."

Holy fuck that's hot.

My cheeks heat in response, along with that place between my legs that's burning right now. He brings his hand down to the bottom of my mini dress, then raises it above my head.

"Have any limits?" he asks, looking at both of us.

Kalie nods her head. "I'm a virgin, and I want to keep it that way. Anything else I'm fine with."

His body stills. "Are you sure you want to do this Kalie? You can stop it anytime, okay?"

The man has a heart. Just fucking great! I think I'm doomed.

She nods her head. "Thanks, Blake, but I'm sure." The look on her face agreeing with her answer.

He removes my bra, sliding his hands over my perky nipples and putting one in his mouth. I throw my head back as the heat from his mouth surrounds one of my most sensitive spots. He comes back up and takes off his cut before pulling his T-shirt from his body showcasing the most defined muscles I've ever seen, without looking too big. He unbuckles his belt and button, leaving them there to hang open while he picks me up and throws me onto the bed with Kalie. He stands at the end looking at both of us with a smirk on his face and starts crawling up the bed to Kalie. She swallows and slides herself down the bed so he's above her, with one fist on each side of her head.

He cocks his head to the side, setting up shop in between her legs. I watch in fascination as he leans down, licking her neck while keeping his eyes locked on mine. My face is on fire at this point, I've never been so fucking turned on in all my life. Biting her ear, he raises her dress above her head. He then makes his way back down to her, pulling off her bra and sucking on her nipples.

I'm going to die a very horny woman.

He looks up at me and grabs my hand, putting it over my pussy before smirking and saying, "Not too much."

My eyes roll back as I begin to pleasure myself while watching the show taking place in front of me. I watch Kalie panting with need as he starts licking down her stomach. Reaching her panties, he pulls them off, throwing them to the side. He looks over, seeing me pleasuring myself before crawling up to me and pulling my panties down to match Kalie's on the floor. Hiking my leg over his shoulder, he begins to blow softly on my pussy while I squeeze my nipples searching for a release.

Looking over to Kalie, she moves in right next to me. Before I can think of anything, I see stars from Blake's tongue creating magic between my thighs.

"Oh my God," I moan. He stops and flips me over me, so I'm straddling his face.

"Ride my tongue."

Looking down at Kalie again I see she's already started taking him deep in her mouth, so I do as he says. I begin to ride his mouth and tongue slowly, feeling his slick wet tongue slide over my clit every two seconds before diving back into my pussy. I do this simultaneously, so I'm working myself up and up until I cannot go any further. When I feel my body starting to reach its maximum peak and I think I can't go any further, Blake grips onto my ass and pushes my pussy flush up against his mouth. This sensation overload makes me thrust rough, hard and fast on his tongue until I'm screaming out in ecstasy. My legs shake as the tremors rip through my body, while I try to slow my breathing down from my orgasm. I swing my leg back over so he can have air, I notice the prick is smiling a boyish smile at me.

He slaps my ass before grabbing Kalie. "Come here, darling." She blushes beet red and I smirk at her. Laying her down, he spreads her legs apart. Just as he's about to take her in his mouth, a phone rings.

"Fuck!" He gets up from the bed, pulling his phone out of his pocket. "I have to answer this. You two carry on if you want," he replies with a smirk.

"Yeah, nope. Not going to happen," I say to him as both Kalie and I laugh. I love her to bits, but there's no way we're doing *that*.

"What?" he snaps down his phone, then a smirk slowly creeps across his lips. "Oh yeah? Is that right, *Ade?*" He chuckles, looking over at Kalie briefly.

"Oh, trust me, brother. I'm almost one hundred percent positive that she'll be worth it. Looking at the position she's in now. All pink and wet, waiting for my tongue to slide all over that sweet pussy. Oh, and did I mention that she's a virgin?" He laughs and throws his phone down to the bed.

"I can't believe you told some random guy about my virginity," Kalie berates.

"Trust me, baby, he's not going to be some random guy for much longer."

"Get up, darling. You're apparently off limits," he says, throwing her clothes at her.

"What? No way! Says who!" Kalie replies.

I look between the two of them and ask, "Ade?" I laugh. "I knew it. Maybe he should've thought about that before he started sucking face with walking chlamydia."

Blake looks over to me and pauses before shaking his head.

Not ten minutes later Ade kicks open the door, storms over to Kalie and picks her up. He looks over at Blake and growls, actually growls, like a hot caveman.

"Oh my God. What are you doing?" she protests as he begins walking out the door. "Seriously? You're not going to grunt or bang on your chest too, are you?"

"This is not over." He storms out with a pissed off looking Kalie hanging over his shoulder, protesting.

I get up out of the bed, throwing Blake's shirt on and go get a drink. "Well, that was interesting," I mumble while taking sips of my orange juice and making my way back to the bed. "Does he usually play caveman with all the girls?"

Blake laughs. "Definitely not. Ade is emotionless where women are concerned. His level of fucks given is so far is below zero, he could ice you with one stare..." he pauses for a second before continuing, "But when he does care about someone, he cares savagely."

"What about you?" I ask, peeking under my lashes at him.

"What about me?" He props himself up, leaning on one arm while looking at me.

"Are you emotionless?"

He laughs, taking a swig of his drink. "When it comes to relationships, yes. I'm just not interested."

I nod my head in approval. "Same here."

He tilts his head in surprise. "You're not interested in a relationship?"

I shake my head and swallow. "Nope, not at all. Not ever. At least, not yet anyway."

He places his drink down and pulls at my legs, dragging me down the bed. "No strings attached?" he asks with one eyebrow raised.

"Definitely, no strings attached."

He then lays a perfect kiss on my lips before pulling me out of his T-shirt while licking my neck, coming along my jaw and kissing me hard again. My whole body comes back to life as if he's just hit a switch for my body.

I should probably defuse that switch...

I pull at his pants until his cock springs free. Taking him in my hand, I begin to pump as he grinds into my touch. By this point, I'm needy for him all over again. He slides my panties down before reaching for a condom and rolling it down his long thick length. *And holy shit is it a length*. I thought Jesse was big, but Blake is a monster.

He makes his way back on top of me and I wonder briefly how the hell it's supposed to fit, then he slams into me before I can express my thoughts. I scream out in pleasure, gripping his shoulder blades as he pulls out of me slowly, before pushing back into me at a slow and steady pace.

He's teasing me with his cock.

"Blake, please...harder." He groans against my neck, before slamming into me at full force. This is not sex. Sex does not even cover what this is. This is pure, rough, fucking. Nothing more, and nothing less. Pulling out of me, he flips me onto my stomach, slaps my ass and descends back inside me again. He's lifting my ass up into the air and pulling my hair back, going at a perfect pace. Feeling the head of his cock massage my g-spot, he's hitting it without missing every time. With every deep thrust, I climb higher and higher, and just when I think I'm done climbing the orgasm mountain, he slams into me with one last thrust and I'm lost in the pleasure from his dick. The evidence of my orgasm running all over his pulsing shaft. My body shakes from the after effects, as I flop down on the bed with him sliding in next to me.

"Do you have a cigarette?" I ask him, lying on my back.

"Say what?" he asks in shock. I roll my eyes. I thought him of all people wouldn't judge my secret habit. I only smoke when I drink or after great sex, and *that* was amazingly great sex.

"Don't start, biker man."

He laughs before shaking his head. "I wasn't going to. I have a cigarette, but it's not the tobacco kind?"

I nod my head in approval. "Even better, blaze it up." He reaches for his *'cigarette'* while turning on his sound dock. Metallica's *'Fade to Black'* starts flowing through the speakers.

I think I'm in love with him.

"You like Metallica?" I ask, closing my eyes while I take in the sound of my favorite band. He looks at me as if I have three heads.

"Like, is an understatement, babe. Rock is my forte," he responds around the green stick in his mouth. I jump onto him instinctively, so I'm straddling him.

Taking the joint out of his mouth and putting it in my own, I take a hard pull. Maybe I hit it a little too hard because now I'm choking my ass off.

He laughs. "Easy babe, that shit isn't your average Mary Jane." He lays me back down onto my back while looking down at me. I'm almost certain I'm high enough, my heavy eyes giving me away.

"You got me at Metallica," I whisper, looking deep into his eyes.

I see something flash over his face before he replaces it with one of his mischievous grins. "You impress me, you know?" he chuckles, taking another puff as the song kicks upbeat. "Not many girls know and appreciate good old school rock. They all listen to new trash on the radio."

I nod in agreement before propping my head on my hand so I'm facing him sideways. "Right, I feel the exact same way. My dad had me listening to Guns & Roses as a new-born baby apparently. My mom said that he used it as my lullaby," I reply while taking the joint back from him so I can assault my throat again with another puff of the strong ganja.

"Which song did he play to you?" he asks. I look to him, blowing out a large cloud of smoke.

Anyone would think you were a pro. Slow it down Snoop Lion.

"'*Don't Cry,*'" I reply, smiling at the memory of how my great my dad was—until he started dating a girl I went to school with.

"Nice, it's a good song," he says, putting out the rest of our illegal substance before jumping into bed with me. I realize that I'm a lot more tired than I thought.

"Will Kalie be okay? Ade isn't a serial killer?" He pulls me under his arm, laying kisses on my head.

It means nothing Vicky, don't think into it.

"How many do you get before it's classed as a serial killer?"

I shove him in the chest. "That's not funny, but I'd say around five."

He laughs. "Then no, he's not a serial killer."

I relax a little until he adds, "He's much worse."

I shoot up off the bed. Hearing him sigh. I turn to face him, but before I can say anything, he beats me to it.

"Babe, Ade's a good man. Under all the alpha-domineering-caveman shit. He obviously has some weird crap going on with your friend that I've never ever seen before, and I've known Ade since we were in diapers. Chill." He pulls me back down under his arm. "Get some sleep." I relax into his big warm arms and it's not long before I drift off into quiet darkness.

"Nooo, stop," I exclaim, waving my hand around my face. I hear a deep chuckle and remember where I am.

"Blake, shut the curtains. So not cool."

"Get up, baby. I got some shit to sort and Kalie's here."

I shoot up off the bed. "Where is she?"

Fuck, I hope she's okay.

"She's in the living room. I put my number in your phone, text me when you get home."

I look at him while wiping my hair out of my face in an unladylike way.

Who am I kidding! There's not a ladylike bone in my size six body.

"Is this going to be weird? I mean, I know you guys live in Westbeach—" he cuts me off.

"No, not at all," he says, pulling me in for a kiss.

"Text me, yeah?"

I nod. "Yep, will do."

He starts to walk out the door and I'm still perving at his ass when Kalie walks in.

"Shit, are you okay?" I ask her. She blushes bright red and my face goes serious.

"Oh shit…" *Fucking bikers.* "Kalie! A hot as fuck biker plays the caveman card on you and you give it up the first night?" She laughs while flopping onto the bed with me. I continue, "Poor ex-boyfriend, slumming it for years and he never gets any. But Ade-bad-boy-biker comes along and suddenly your panties disappear." By this point, she's in fits of laughter.

"I know, I'm a terrible person. But oh my God, Vicky!" she says, her eyes drifting off into dreamland.

I look over at her and ask, "That good, huh?" I begin to gather up my stuff.

"Really, *really* good. Shit."

"You going to see him again?"

She looks down at her hands and says, "Um…I don't know. I think it was just a one-night thing."

Not a good sign.

"That okay with you?"

She looks up to me. "Yep! Yeah, that's cool."

I can see it's definitely not. Kalie can lie through her mouth, but her eyes tell a thousand stories.

The girl is deep, and she's not cut out for the complications that come with sex.

"All right then, let's go and get some lunch."

Sitting at the local beach lunch bar, I order bacon, eggs, pancakes, and waffles. Kalie looks over to me.

"No fair, Vick. Just because your weight goes nowhere, some of us have to actually watch what we eat." I have no idea what she's talking about. She has an amazing curvy figure—all small waist, hourglass hips, nice big booty sitting behind her, and these boobs that not even money could buy. She's one of the most beautiful girls I've ever seen.

"Kalie, you're an idiot. You're totally banging and you need to know it."

She looks at me while sipping her coffee. "Banging shouldn't jiggle."

I roll my eyes, all that would jiggle on her petite five-foot-four frame would be her natural bubble ass and boobs.

"So, what's Blake like?" she asks me, in between eating a banana.

"He's male, that's what he is. No commitments and all that."

She sits forward, putting her banana down. "What's '*all that*'?" she asks.

"It's when you know there's not going to be anything more to us but sex, and that's fine with me. I like playing."

She giggles. "Yeah, you do!" And we both start laughing as memories from last night came flooding through my brain.

"I thought we should throw a little party tonight? Invite some people. We could hand out some flyers today down at the beach?"

Kalie nods her head, looking excited. "Oh, good idea."

After paying for our food, we make our way back to my car. Pulling my door open, I say, "Let's go and make some invites." Kalie squeals in excitement before getting into the driver's seat.

Two hours later and we are looking down at our invites. I have to give it to us, we've done a pretty rad job. We get into our bikinis and notice it's still only 1:00 p.m., so we have heaps of time to hand out the invites and come back to get ready. We slide into my car before setting off to the main beach.

"Remind me to stop at the store or I'll forget," I say to Kalie as she laughs at my honesty. "Have you heard from Blake?" she asks, glancing out in front of us.

"Nope, I'll text him my number later."

After Kalie's comment, I can't get Blake out of my mind. I do want another round, but not tonight. Tonight I just want to have fun. Pulling up to the car park, I push open my door.

"Invites to hotties only," I say, wiggling my eyebrows.

We step onto the beachfront where there are people everywhere and begin handing out the invites to anyone and everyone, getting a huge response. With it being spring break, you can only imagine how keen everyone is for a good old house party.

We did not have to stay very long, an hour later and we were at the store stocking up.

"Okay, we'll just get some kegs, pre-mixers and a whole bunch of finger food."

Kalie nods as we go our separate ways to purchase all the things we need. It takes us forty-five minutes all up, but at least we're all ready to go. I clap my hands together in excitement.

Walking through my front door, I realize that I almost forgot to text Blake. So I pull out my phone and send him a quick text message.

> Me: *Hey biker man it's Vick. This is my number.*

How original Vicky, geez you're so intelligent.

> Blake: *Took you long enough. What you doing?*
> Me: *Just setting up, having a little…um…thing tonight.*
> Blake: *Thing???*
> Me: *Yeah, it wouldn't be a big, bad, biker sort of…thing.*
> Blake: *Have fun.*
> Me: *Did I piss you off?*
> Me: *???*

After waiting ten minutes for a reply, I decide to put my phone down. Here come all the confusing parts about have a *no strings attached* relationship.

"Fucking great," I mumble to myself as Kalie walks in.

"You okay?" she asks, looking up at me.

"Yeah, yeah," I assure her, waving my hands away. "Let's just get pretty."

It's 11:15 p.m. and my parents' huge beach mansion is chock-a-block with people everywhere. Kalie and I are very much thoroughly drunk. We're both wearing bikinis, with a belly chain coming around my neck, and sitting on my waistline. Kalie chose heels, and I chose Nike high tops. I'm tall enough as it is and if I wear heels, I'll look like a Sasquatch. *Tall girl problems.* Walking around, I'm being acquainted with everyone and it's fun. I'm in my element and I end up having a whole lot of new numbers in my phone book.

Bet Alaina wishes she came now.

I'm rounding the corner after coming in from the pool, and I smash straight into a hard chest.

"Holy shit, I'm so—" my slurring stops as I look up to a mischievous looking Blake.

"I should ask how you know my address, but I'm too horny to care."

He tilts his head to the side, in the way I'm growing to love. "If you were horny, why didn't you text me?"

I laugh at his cockiness. "Because I was obviously open to a new selection of toys tonight." His eyes narrow, giving me the sexiest evils I've ever seen. This man is all play, no stay, and my body could not crave him more if I tried.

He picks me up laughing, so I wrap my legs around his waist while we go smashing into my room. We're kissing and making out like a couple of dogs on heat. He does this to me, I notice. I'm usually bored after one night. Pushing me down onto the bed, he crawls up to me, looking deep into my eyes.

"You can do what you want, Vicky. I don't really care. But when I want you, it's only to be me unless stated otherwise."

Laughing before looking straight back into his eyes. "You mean unless I say it's payback time with one of the hottie-McBiker crew?"

He chuckles. "That's undecided, darling. Now come here."

He drags me down the bed, before ripping off my bikini and getting down to what he does best, giving me earth shattering orgasms.

BLAKE

Once I know Vicky's asleep, I get up out of the bed. There's no way I'm sleeping the night. The first time was a mistake, that won't happen again. I don't know why my lines get blurred with this girl. Walking out of her house and getting onto my bike, I flick a text to Zane.

Me: *Brother, I can't do this for long.*
Zane: *Wait until we've met Alaina. We need our in.*
Me: *Time frame?*
Zane: *When I fucking say so.*

Pushing my phone back in my pocket, I'm pissed off with my best friend. Getting on my bike and bringing her to life, I roll back before taking off down the driveway and out the front gate. I'm unsure of where I'm heading, but I end up at the beach front. Turning off my bike and getting off, I walk down to the shoreline wondering why the fuck I can't get this girl out of my head. I already know I've mastered some sort of shitty feelings for her, they're not deep or anything right now, but they're fucking there. Now that I'm aware of these so-called feelings, I can stop them. All I can do is hope that she doesn't *swing* the way I like to and runs away from me.

Me: *Want to do something tonight?*

Vicky: *Oh, the night leaver. Did the bed bugs bite?*
Me: *Something did...*
Vicky: *Sounds interesting. Do tell?*
Me: *Not important. You free tonight?*
Vicky: *I can be. What's the plan?*
Me: *Surprise. Dress in something tight that flashes your tits.*
Vicky: *I can do that :)*

Putting my phone back in my pocket, I make my way back to my bike thinking to myself that this plan has to work. There's no way she'd be interested in me if she knew this is how I party.

Getting back to the hotel room, I run into Ade.

"How's Vicky doing?" he asks me. Knowing the bitch has every alarm bell that screams, *'Don't fuck with me or I will slit your throat in your sleep.'*

"She's not. I'm taking her to Sinsation."

Ade stops in his tracks before laughing, "You really want to go down that road with her?"

Obviously fucking not.

"I don't really have a choice, Ade. What's going on with you and Kalie anyway?"

He stills while his body drops. "Nothing, it's done. She's way too good for me."

I could have fucking told him that.

"Yeah, she is."

Ade is a virgin's worst nightmare. She should have stayed with me. He nods his head before heading out the doors.

Unpacking all my shit out of my pockets and putting it all on the bedside table, I huff out in confusion before sitting on the bed.

What the fuck have you gotten yourself into Blake?

Picking up my phone, I dial my sister. I haven't heard from her in a while because she's in New York, slaying the fashion world. She's exactly what you'd expect in an annoying little sister, but I love her more than anything.

"Blake!" she screams down the phone line, and I instantly smile.

"Hey Speedy, how's things going?" Speedy is her nickname, she earned it because the girl is a car fanatic. Anything fast with four wheels she knows about, but looking at her you wouldn't know—she's all blonde hair and baby-faced.

"Good, I miss you so much."

I need to hear her voice. After our parents died in a car accident along with Zane's dad, it's just been her and me. She's all I have and care about aside from my club. “I miss you, too. Come up here soon. Will you?”

“I’ll try and get there soon as possible. I love you.”

“I love you, too,” I reply before hanging up the phone.

Looking around my room, I’m reminded of Vicky. Fuck this girl is spectacular. She’s not like other girls, she’s not clingy or needy and she doesn’t have one of those annoying fucking whiney voices most girls have when they want you to lay the world at their feet. Vicky is relaxed, outgoing and down for almost anything.

We’ll see if that will still apply after tonight.

Getting up, I make my way to the shower, scrubbing away any thoughts that I had of a tall, leggy brunette. Once I’m dressed, I get a call from Zane.

“What can I do for you, brother?”

“We have an issue. Devil’s Soldiers know we’re on their turf, I’m going to meet with Tick now.”

I did wonder how long it would last before they found out we were here.

“Where? I’ll meet you there?”

“21 on Fifth, see you there at ten.”

Riding out there, I know we're good. There's no way Tick will start a war with us, especially if it's uncalled for. We've maintained a good business relationship with him for the past three years since Zane took over from his old man. Not only is Zane not to be fucked with in any way, but he's book smart as well. He managed to pull our club out of a lot of shit that our fathers left before the accident.

Pulling up at the industrial building, I see Zane and Ade getting off their bikes.

"This doesn't look suspicious at all." I'm being honest here, it sounds like a bit of a setup.

"He won't do anything, trust me. He doesn't want to go down that road. We have an understanding," Zane assures me as we begin walking into the building.

The door creaks as we push it open. In front of us is an enormous empty space. We watch Tick and his main three men sitting next to him at a table. Zane walks ahead of Ade and me, so we follow suit.

"Zane." Tick nods his head.

Tick is around thirty-four and he's young. Zane is the youngest of all the presidents in our area that we know of. But the man has been raised and bred for this purpose and this purpose only, making him the most feared man in the MC world. I chuckle to myself in my thoughts.

One of the other men to the side of Tick laughs aloud. "If it isn't Sinful Club's pretty boy."

I fucking hate him instantly.

Zane turns his head to the voice before looking back at Tick. "You going to shut up your BumBoy or should I do it for you?"

Tick glares at the man, making him sit back down on his seat. "So, to what do we owe the pleasure of having you boys on our streets?"

"We have an assignment. The required asset is currently on your turf…for now."

"Yeah, all right," he says, leaning back into his chair while lighting a cigarette.

"You thought about my offer?"

I look over to Zane with a questioning glance. It's the first time I've heard about an *offer*.

"Yeah, I'm taking it in for a vote when I get back to Westbeach."

Tick nods before looking over to me. "Blake, this is Treasure." He nods over to the lippy fucker sitting at his left side with a disgusted look on his face.

"And? Is that supposed to be of some relevance to me, Tick?"

He laughs, looking back at Treasure, and then looking back to me with an arched eyebrow. "I guess not, no. But he's from my Brooklyn Chapter. Just patched in with us."

I shrug because I have no idea what the fuck this man is on about. Yet, his face is saying that he's waiting for me to click.

"Are we done here? I have shit to do."

"We're done here."

Walking back out the way we came, Zane looks over to me."

What the hell was that comment about Treasure?"

Shrugging I honestly have no idea. The man didn't look the least bit familiar.

He continues, "I hear you're taking Vicky to Sinsation tonight. That a good idea?"

"Yeah, gonna see what this girl can do."

Zane shakes his head laughing. He knows exactly what I'm thinking.

CHAPTER 4

VICKY

After Blake up and left me in the middle of the night, it put my head into perspective.

You're in this for a good time, not a long time Vicky, I chant to myself as I put on a short deep purple dress that, as he said, "shows off my tits." Not only did that little comment make me feel like one of his club whores, but also it reminded me of exactly why I shouldn't be interested in this man on any level, despite our chemistry. Putting on my stilettos, I make my way into the kitchen to down a couple of shots before this night begins. Because, in all honesty, I have no idea what he has in store for me.

Three shots later, I hear the loud rumble of his bike. Looking up, I breathe in and out slowly, trying to calm my nerves. Grabbing my clutch off the marble counter, I begin to make my way out. Just as I'm walking out the front door, I see him, and my whole body buzzes to life.

Holy fuck Vicky, just what have you gotten yourself into?

He's sitting on his bike in dark denim jeans, a black T-shirt with his cut over the top, combat boots and his dark blond hair sitting up all over the place on his head. I smile while blushing.

Victoria Abraham does not blush.

"Um...I can't ride that with this on?" I state, looking down at my dress.

"Trust me, darling. It's been done before."

Thanks for that! Really, that's just what I want to hear.

"Hmmm, okay then."

I walk to him unsure. He's wearing his mischievous smile. This man is all play, he doesn't have a serious bone in his body. Taking the offered helmet, I jump behind him pulling up my skirt, feeling a cold breeze whisk up my legs and skim over my sex. A slight moan escapes my lips, so quietly I *think* no one heard.

Blake tips his head around, looking at me sideways. "You moan like that again, and I'll lock you up for a week," he says as he starts up his immaculate gloss black Harley. I feel the rumble pulse under me, making me itchy for a release.

This is fucking torture.

Placing my hands around his waist, he reaches behind and grips onto my knees, pulling me flush up against his back. *Fuck. My. Life.* At this point, I'm biting down so hard on my bottom lip that I'm pretty sure I've drawn blood. Wrapping my arms around him—which do not reach all the way—he pulls out of my driveway. With this being my first time riding on a motorcycle, I'm anxious and feeling vulnerable. It's not like you're wrapped in sheets of metal to protect you. There's just my bare lanky legs and the gravel. The thought makes me grip onto Blake tighter, and I notice his body tense up.

Oops, maybe I'm not allowed to touch too much, I think. Reminding myself of how he rejected Kalie's hands from coming up his neck.

Nope, there's no way I'm doing 'several shades of fucked up' with a biker. Fuck that.

Our ride there is long. Instead of my previous issue of having the rumble of the bike vibrate in my core, I'm now having an issue about not feeling my ass at all. And I'm almost one hundred percent sure my hair is going to be a disaster. As much as I love being this close to Blake, I think for future dressy dates I'll be opting for a car.

Dates? You're dreaming, Vicky.

We pull into what looks like a nightclub. It's entirely painted red on the outside and has two black doors as the entry point, and they look like the gates to hell if you ask me. I look over to him as I try to brush my hair back into some sort of order.

"Are you dragging me into your lair?" I laugh nervously.

"Something like that." He smirks, taking hold of my hand and making our way through the gates of hell. I look around to what appears to be a typical bar. Following Blake to the main bar, I let him order the drinks while examining my surroundings. There seems to be many little hidden areas, and when I look a little closer at the people that are here, I notice they're all couples.

"What did you say this bar was?" I ask, taking my drink and slamming it down fast. All my senses are telling me that I may not be cut out for this.

"I didn't. But look around Vicky, what's your body telling you?" he whispers into my ear, igniting that same flame that always sparks when Blake's around. I look back into his eyes, admiring the dark depths of the most expressive eyes I've ever seen.

"This is a swinger's bar, isn't it?"

He pounds back his whiskey before ordering us another. Leaning back on the bar, he tilts his head to the side, scratching his chin. "Indeed it is, and it's mine."

Whoa, hold the fuck up.

"I'm sorry, what? You own a swinger's bar?"

He nods his head, clenching his jaw. "Yeah. I do. Come." He begins to lead me to the back, walking past the little *private* sections, and I see a few live porn shows happening right there on display for anyone to peek into. Once we get to the back of the bar, we reach a metal door that has a card slider next to it. Blake pulls out a card and swipes it through, leading me to an elevator. When the doors close, I turn my head to him.

"So, you're taking me to a sex party?" I ask, folding my arms in front of myself. He leans up against the wall with his hands in his pockets while he looks at me with such intensity. I feel as though he's cracking my soul open right in front of me. A few pulses of his jaw later, the doors open and he pulls me out into the long hallway. I yank my hand back out of his grasp.

"Blake? You're going to have to give me something," I say, stopping in my tracks as I look around nervously.

"Do you trust me, Vicky?" he asks while reaching for my hand.

"No. No, I definitely do not trust you right now Blake. I'm not one of those females that are willing to put all their trust into the first guy that makes her extremely sex driven."

He laughs at me. *Asshole.*

"I'm serious, Blake. I'm not a *'ride or die'* kind of chick. I have questions. Like where are we riding to? Why do I have to die? Can't I just be a stay home—You fuck me when you want and call me later kind of chick?"

A slow but panty dropping smirk comes on full HD display across his face. He steps up to me, taking my face in his hands and kisses me on the lips.

"You're so fucking different. I hate it."

"Thanks. *I think,*" I reply as I clutch my hand into his.

"Come on, it's play time."

I don't think I want to play with him. His toys scare me.

Once we reach the door, he reaches into his back pocket and pulls out a blindfold.

Where did that come from, MacGyver?

"This is an elite club, Vicky. Only the best of the best come here, out of complete discretion..." he pauses for a second before continuing, "Just trust me, baby. I wouldn't do anything to hurt you." I glance down at the black blindfold, lined with lace and then look back into his eyes.

Those damn eyes, they had me at day one.

Nodding my head in approval, my hormones are obviously doing all the thinking for me, because my brain has left the building. Maybe I left it somewhere in Westbeach. I seem to be making a lot of out of this world decisions since being here.

This is all Jesse's fault.

He comes up behind me and places the blindfold over my eyes while slowly kissing wet kisses down the side of my neck. I feel his lips brush up against my ear before he lightly bites down on it. Hearing a door open, all I can see is blackness. Then I hear music playing in the background, with people talking. At least, I think they're talking.

Blake brings his lips back to my ear. "There are three couples in this room Vicky, and all the girls are blindfolded. Understood?"

I swallow loudly, my head is screaming—*no, this is definitely not good,* but my instincts to explore are telling me, *this is very fucking good.* "Okay."

He proceeds to lead me into what I guess is a room. I hear the voices go quiet and Blake's grip on my arm lets go.

"Strip," is the next thing I hear come out of his mouth.

"What?" I whisper, thinking that maybe he could still hear me.

He wants me to strip in front of three other men?

He's definitely only in this for a good time only. I swallow down my thoughts before beginning this *'show'* for him.

BLAKE

"Strip," I demand as she stands in the middle of the room. I look over at the other three men that are sitting here about to get the show of their life. Vicky's body is out of this world. She slowly unzips the back of her tight dress, then it drops and pools at her feet. Standing there with her hair around her face, falling perfectly past her tits. The blindfold is sitting on her eyes and she's in the sexiest lace getup I've ever seen. She looks fucking phenomenal. I take a long drag of my beer, trying to swallow the jealousy I can feel creeping up inside me.

This has never happened before. I fucking never get jealous during a scene.

I can't feel.

This is hopefully what's going to stop me from feeling for her. Ryder gets up and starts to make his way to her. Ryder's been a part of Sinstation since the beginning. However, no one can know that he attends these parties. Ryder Oakley is the lead singer of Twisted Transistor, who are the most famous rock band out there today. I know if she saw him she'd be begging him to put his dick down her throat, like every other girl in this universe. So the blindfold stays. He proceeds to make his way to her, and my uneasiness continues to grow. *Pull yourself together, Blake.*

VICKY

My nervousness is getting the best of me as my breathing picks up. I feel someone move next to me and whisper in my ear, "You all right with this babe? You look a little nervous." His voice is smooth, but at the same time it's hard. That might just be the sexiest voice I've ever heard.

I swallow again, turning my head toward the voice. "I'm good. Can't say I've ever done anything like this before, but there's a first for everything."

His hand wraps around my arm softly, turning me to him. They feel strong and easily wrap around my whole upper arm. He runs his smooth lips over mine softly. Not kissing, just sliding them over, probably testing my interest and I respect that. I can feel two lip rings next to each other on his lips.

Well, hello there.

His hand wraps behind the back of my neck, and he bends down pushing my lips against his, and then lightly bites down on my lower lip. A moan slips softly from my lips as he brushes his hands down the front of my body, running them slowly over my breasts and stomach area. I hear a hiss come from somewhere in the room, and I'm almost sure it came from Blake. This shit must *really* turn him on. A hand reaches behind my back, unclasping my bra in one swift move. I feel a breeze skim past my nipples, making them come to life instantly.

"Shit Blake! She's much better than the last girl you brought in here."

I stop and my mouth sets into a hard line. "Wait! What? You do this a lot?" I say to the air because I have no idea where Blake is.

I hear him reply from a small distance in front of me. "You're not special, darling. Of course, I have." His response makes me clench my jaw together. *Fucking prick.*

Turning back to the apparently keen man in front of me, I whisper to him and him only, "Can I see you?" There's a pause before I feel his hands come up to my blindfold.

"Ryder," Blake growls in warning from where he's sitting.

"She wants to see who it is touching her Blake, since when is that an issue? They always have the option to choose, and if we don't like it we can walk out. I want her to see me." That voice is so alluring, I hope the man who owns it is just as sexy. He begins pulling off the blindfold, making my hair slowly fall back. I narrow my eyes as they adjust to the dimly lit room, finally opening them to focus properly. I cannot believe what I see.

Oh my fucking God!

"Oh my God, no freaking way!" I say, throwing my hand up to my mouth.

"Ryder Oakley? *The* Ryder Oakley, from Twisted Transistor?"

He smirks. "The one and only."

I'm star struck. There's no way I was just kissing Ryder freaking Oakley.

Kalie is going to flip the fuck out.

"Is it completely inappropriate to ask you for your autograph right now?"

He laughs. "I can sign it in between your legs?"

I blush bright beetroot red. "Okay, deal."

Holy shit.

He smiles, putting the blindfold back on my eyes, and I let him. Now I know what I'm dealing with, I'm only too happy to have him between my legs on any occasion.

Please, I've had worse.

He brings his lips back to mine kissing me deep and hard before running his tongue down my neck to my breasts and then pulling them both into his warm mouth. I bring my arms up around his neck, stepping closer to him. Thinking this is precisely what Blake wants. This is how he plays. It is twisted and sick, but this…I can live with.

Running my hands through his hair, his face drags down to my apex. He picks me up, wrapping my legs around his face and dropping me onto a bed.

Where the hell did the bed come from?

Spreading my legs wide, he begins to draw a pattern in my inner thigh. I giggle because it tickles and I know what he has just done. *Hot*. I feel the roughness of his jeans brush up against me making me widen my legs even more, letting him in gladly.

I still have a sickening feeling in the pit of my stomach, though. Once again, I have to remind myself that Blake doesn't care, this is what he does and that I'm not special.

His words, not mine.

I feel a bulge pushing and grinding into me. Pushing myself back up to him, it feels like it's just me and him, no one else. The next time this blindfold comes off, I need to check around the room. I didn't even have a proper look last time to see who's exactly in here.

Shit, sloppy move Vicky.

"I'll put some music on," I hear Blake say from a short distance away and Avenged Sevenfold's *'Hail to the King'* starts pumping loudly through the speakers, putting my body at ease with every strum of the guitar.

"Put it on repeat," Ryder murmurs into the crook of my neck. These men are going to absolutely annihilate me, and I will love every second of it. Feeling his breath slide down the side of my neck, his voice vibrates on my skin. "You sure you're cool with this? I can take you to a private room where Blake can't shoot daggers at me?"

My face drops at the mention of Blake's name. "It's fine. This was his idea after all. It must be what he wants."

I feel a deep chuckle against my neck. "A revenge fuck? My favorite kind." Before he drags his hands down to my pussy, rubbing me slowly. He starts to pull my panties down my legs, and I can hear moaning coming from somewhere in the room. Something deep, dark and seductive takes over my body, as I let the feeling of uneasiness go and my kinky inner side comes out.

Are those moans coming from Blake? I squash back my thoughts.

If they are, it doesn't bother me. If anything, it turns me on more. What we have is not serious, it's a *twisted game.*

My thoughts are paused as I feel a hot mouth right between my legs. I moan out in complete and utter euphoria as Ryder's five o'clock shadow grazes lightly between my thighs, before bringing himself back up to me. I feel him move off the bed and hear a buckle undo.

Holy shit! I'm so turned on right now it's insane. Who would have known? I kind of dig group sex.

Kneeling back on the bed, I feel him come back down. Nibbling my neck softly, I hear a condom wrapper being opened.

"Ryder," a soft but harsh growl vibrates around the room. In between another girl moaning, I answer back to Blake's growl, "Blake, unless you're going to come join in. You need to shut the fuck up, right now."

I feel Ryder's chest shaking on top of me from his laughing. "Yo, she's a keeper, B."

There's a moment of silence, and then I feel a soft finger run down my cheek. "And you think you can take both Ryder and me?" Blake asks as he pulls his hand away from my cheek.

"Positive."

Way too much confidence Abrahams. No one likes a cocktease.

Blake chuckles, and then I feel the bed dip with another body. I'm swallowing down my nerves as Ryder rolls to the other side of me. The moaning that I was hearing has now stopped, and I hear a "shhh" sound come from someone else in the room.

Great, now I have an audience. I can add porn star to my résumé. Call me Doubles88, because both of these men are packing 8er's.

"Ryder? Stay the fuck on your side," Blake sneers.

I hear Ryder laugh. "Don't need to tell me twice."

Fuck, I'm really doing this.

Blake turns my head to him and whispers against my lips, "Take off the blindfold, Vicky."

I swiftly take it off and look at both sexy men sitting on either side of me. I smile and Blake smiles back at me, and I think I melt a little.

Not good at all.

Blake runs his thumb over my bottom lip, before taking me with his mouth. I'm getting lost in Blake's kiss when I feel another hand run over my nipple. I arch my back, wanting more of *everything* when I feel a second set of hands down on me. Getting to work, I reach for Blake first almost as a reflex. Pausing I reach up to Ryder instead, kissing him while Blake makes his way down my legs. I take hold of Ryder's cock and start pumping it slowly, rubbing his wet, slick tip all over with my thumb to add lube. Blake stops, picks me up and flips me over onto my tummy with an added slap to my ass. Now I'm face down, ass up. I hear a condom wrapper rip open while he still plays with my clit from behind, and I find myself pushing into his hand, working myself up. I glance up to Ryder, who's now directly in front of me, so I grab his dick in my hand, beginning to swallow him deep down into my throat. Just as I start licking around him, Blake slams into me from behind in one hard thrust. I scream out from the raw pleasure as Ryder takes my hair, wraps it around his wrist and fucks my mouth. I've never felt so turned on and I never want it to end. My body has other plans though it seems, as a few deep thrusts later, and the evidence of my orgasm is dripping down Blake's thick cock. And a few seconds later, I feel Ryder's cock pulse down my throat, along with Blake's deep inside me. I flop down onto my stomach, physically exhausted. I forgot about our audience, but I do not want to move. I hear both of the boys chuckle as they're pulling their jeans on.

"What?" I ask.

Shit, the sight I have in front of me. Both of them standing there with nothing but their jeans on—it's a sight to see.

"Nothing babe, you're a good time," Ryder replies after pulling his top down.

"Remember that, because it'll be your only time," Blake replies with a hint of humor in his tone.

I look over to the people that are watching us. There are three girls sitting on the huge sofa looking at us. One, I notice, is without a partner and she seems to be sneering with an evil look directed right at me. I get off the bed and put my clothes back on in record time. By the time I'm finished, this girl has drilled holes into my head with her stares.

"Do you have a problem?" I ask her bluntly. I'm in no mood to deal with anyone's shit.

She walks up to me, curling my hair behind my ear until I pull my head away from her. "Oh sweetie, you think Blake cares about you? The only girl he's ever cared about is me." She follows that statement with a laugh, before walking out of the room.

I look over at Blake, who's standing there motionless and emotionless.

"Who was that?" I ask, pointing to the now empty area that *it* was standing in.

One of the other girls comes up to me. “Hi, I’m Megan. I’m with Tommy, the bass player,” she says all bouncy and chirpy while pointing over to him. Tommy is a big gorilla-sized man with long hair. Under other circumstances, I’d talk to her but not right now. Right now I need words with Blake.

“Blake? Who was that?”

Tommy steps in, looking at me. “Corrin, aka Blake’s ex-girlfriend, aka co-owner of this club,” he smirks around the neck of his bottle.

Looking back at Blake, I see his face is still blank, probably expecting me to go one hundred shades of crazy on his ass. Instead, I laugh.

“Blake, chill. At least the bitch saw me naked. I know you have a huge past. I’ll never hold that against you.”

He swings his head around to me, a small, proud smile on his lips. He moves across to me and picks me up, wrapping my legs around his waist. “Are you even real?” he asks as he starts kissing down my neck, moaning.

He just fucking moaned against my neck.

My body is instantly alert and in desperate need of him again.

“Let’s go,” he says as he takes my hand in his.

We’re walking out the door when Ryder yells out, “Vicky? Your phone, darling.”

I walk back over to him and try to take my phone from his hand, but he doesn't give it to me straight away. Instead, he looks deep into my eyes and smirks.

Jesus, I've seen enough hot men to last me a lifetime…in my spank bank they go.

"There's an extra number in there," he says, letting my phone go and winking at me.

I turn around and move to walk out the door, trying not to think too much into his comment.

"You good?" Blake asks as we're walking back outside.

"Yep, I'm good. So tell me, is this going to be a regular occurrence for us?"

He laughs as we reach his bike. "Do you want it to be?"

I take my helmet that he's holding out to me. "Maybe, we'll see."

"Do you need to be anywhere?" he asks, getting onto his bike.

"Nope." He smiles while starting up his bike. I swing my leg over and hang on.

I think I'm finally getting the hang of this.

We are on the outskirts of Westbeach when we pull up to a high surveillance gate. He gets off and types in a pin before getting back onto his bike and pulling us into a huge, and I mean *huge* house. It has a massive five-car garage to the right side.

Holy shit, it's beautiful.

Cutting the engine, I get off and look around.

"Wait! Is this your house?" I ask kind of shocked.

"Yeah, she's mine. I built her from the ground up," he replies while fishing his keys out of his pocket.

"You actually built this?" Maybe I misheard. This man is a biker after all.

"Yeah, and hired the boys."

"Zane and Ade?" I ask.

He laughs while pushing opening the door. "Definitely not. The only thing Ade can build is a weapon." He continues, "The boys that work for me Vicky, I own Rendon Construction." I raise an eyebrow, realizing I'd stereotyped him and now I feel shit.

"I had no idea. It's amazing in here."

The décor is all very bachelor, as I would expect from Blake. I follow him down a long hallway that leads to a sunken room. You need to step down three steps to get to the door. Opening it, I notice it's a gaming room—a gigantic gaming room. The entire left side of the wall is lined with old arcade games. There's a pool table sitting in the middle, with a large screen television and surround sound system. To the right there's a giant L-shaped sofa and huge floor to ceiling glass doors that open out to a wraparound porch area and backyard. I can see there's a bar right outside the doors, making it the perfect entertainment flow for men. He walks over to the bar fridge pulling out two beers before walking back over to me. I take a drink and point to the pool table.

"You play?" I ask, deciding I want to play a game.

"Do you?" he asks, with a cocky smirk on his lips while taking a drink.

"I'm a keen learner, and just *love* doing first-time activities," I tease, tilting my head to the side and taking another large swig of my drink.

"I'll set us up." He walks over to the table and places all the balls into the triangle, lining it up on the dot. He passes me a cue stick. "I'll break."

I laugh. "Okay then Hercules, you do the honors."

He throws me a second glance, his eyes slightly narrowed. "The slick shit that comes out of your mouth fucking gets me. You're different, Abrahams."

"Stop wasting time and break the balls, Blake. The sooner you do, is the sooner I get to lick yours." Now I feel like tormenting him. If he thinks the stuff I say out loud is bad, he should hear the stuff I keep to myself. My inner dialogue is terrible sometimes. After laughing, he leans down, hitting the balls and sinking little heads.

This man has no idea.

After getting two more in, it's my turn. He walks up behind me, pushing his pelvis into my ass. I immediately notice his thick bulge while showing me how to line up and shoot.

"When you think it's lined up, slide the stick in with force behind you."

Hmmm, much like his fucking skills.

I pull back with no help from him whatsoever and shoot the first one in clean. Then I move to the next ball, shooting that one in also. Five balls later and I slip. I look up to him and he's smirking at me, with surprise written all over his face.

"Where did you learn to play like that?"

I shrug my shoulders. "Beginners luck, maybe?" I answer sarcastically, before putting him out of his misery. "I have three brothers, Blake. While other girls were playing with dolls, I was playing on four wheelers and learning how to create smoke from tires. No big deal." He looks at me, stunned.

"It's a very fucking big deal," he says, with a smile.

Putting the cue down, he makes his way over to me. I step back, shaking my head.

"Oh no, big boy. I need my sleep." Tilting his head to the side, he chuckles while his eyes turn dark with need and mischief. I take this as my cue to run. To where? I do not know. I scream out and begin to run out the room. I spare a quick look behind me and see him chasing me.

"Oh baby, I love the chase. Bad move."

I scream, trying to dodge him and find a room to hide in. Just as I round the corner ready to make a run for it upstairs, he lifts me up from behind and play bites all over my neck.

"Blake! No fair. You know the ins and outs of this house."

He laughs, setting me back down. "Come on, bedtime Grandma."

BLAKE

I wake up to find Vicky not in bed, but the smell of bacon and eggs assaults my senses, instantly making me feel hunger, *and not just for food*. Throwing on my jeans, I make my way downstairs to find Vicky flipping bacon, pancakes, and eggs. Leaning against the doorway, I watch her until she senses that I'm there.

"You know, it's rude to stare," she says smiling, with her hair all up in a messy bun, dancing around in nothing but one of my SS shirts.

"Don't give a fuck, babe. I can stare at you all day."

She blushes before getting back to work. "Sit down, Blake. I think I know my way around here now." I follow orders, sitting down at the breakfast bar.

After eating breakfast, I pop our dishes into the sink. "When are you heading back to Westbeach?" I ask, turning around and leaning on the sink.

"I've got to head back tomorrow. I've got a few things to line up and do." I make my way back to the table. Sitting down, I pull her on top of me so she's sitting on my lap and take an inhale of her sweet scent. *God, I love that smell.*

"Blake? My lines are getting blurred."

I instantly snap my head away from her neck. "What do you mean?"

She stands from my lap, looking unsure of her next words. "I...I don't know. No commitments, right? So can we see other people?"

Yeah, not going to happen, *ever.* As long as she's a part of my world, I cannot imagine ever wanting anyone else.

"Why are you asking this? Do you have someone else lined up for when I'm not around?" I ask, deadly serious, looking into her eyes ready for whatever answer she gives me.

"No. Not off the top of my head anyway. But should the opportunity arise, I just want to make sure we're on the same page."

I clench my jaw a couple times before I reply, "Yes, we're both free to see other people Vicky." I get back up and turn to her. I'm annoyed as fuck at the very real possibility that she could see someone else next week, and I cannot do jack shit about it. "Get dressed, I'll take you back," I say, walking out and leaving her standing there dumbfounded.

The truth is, at this very moment, she fucking owns my world. That's something she'll never know, though. I did *not* expect it to happen, and I definitely did *not* want it to happen, but it has. Now, I need to put some distance between us because that girl in there, makes me feel things that scare the shit out of me. Once I get back into my room, I feel my phone ring in my pocket.

"Got an issue, brother. Someone shot us up last night and we have an idea who that might be."

"Fuck, I'll be there as soon as."

I know we can't discuss this type of shit over the phone. My questions will need to wait until I get there.

"Where are you?" Zane asks while I'm throwing some new clothes on.

"At home. Be there soon."

Throwing the phone back into my bag, I look over to the door and see Vicky dressed in her clothes. "You ready?" I ask.

She nods. So we head downstairs and out the door, back on my bike, and set off on the highway.

Pulling up to Vicky's house I don't turn off my bike, I'm just waiting for her to get off so I can leave.

She passes me the helmet. "Are we okay? Did I say something to piss you off?" she asks.

I shrug because I'm still mad at her question from earlier. "Have a safe trip back, Vick."

Once she slides off the bike, I pull out of her driveway leaving her standing there with obvious questions. I'm a prick and I know that, but it fucks me off knowing that she's been the only girl that gets to me.

I'm making my way back to the hotel when I pull up. I notice Ade and Zane walking down the stairs, with Ade laughing. I knew I should've killed him in his sleep when I had the chance. "What's so funny, fucker?"

He shakes his head still laughing. "Oh, nothing. Just that you're pussy-whipped."

I throw him a disgusted look. "Fuck up, Ade. You don't know shit."

I look to Zane. "What's the issue?"

"It seems your little sister likes bikers."

What the fuck?

"Say what now? No way. She's way too fancy for that shit."

Zane shakes his head and then lights up a cigarette, which I've not seen him do in a long time.

"Nah brother, she's been seeing Treasure. But before him there was Sinner, who's apparently none too happy about her being with Treasure. While he was stalking the place down, having a Treasure hunt, he found out about us being here. The dumb fucker is obviously uneducated on how we roll because I'm about to blow his fucking brains out." Taking a long inhale of his cigarette, I see it has him on edge. This entire stupid fucking *'project'* has him on edge.

"Fuck. Let me call her real quick."

Fucking stupid little shit.

She picks up on the third ring. "Shit! Blake, I'm so sorry—"

"Fucking save it, Phoebe. What the fuck is going on? And why the fuck are you playing with fucking bikers?"

"Don't play dumb. You and Dad were both a part of an MC. You really think I was going to like a suit and tie man?"

"Well, I had fucking hoped you would. Fuck sake! Do you have any idea what this shit has caused? Not just for us, but for the Devils too?"

She sighs down the phone. "I know, I'm sorry."

"What can you tell me about him?"

"Sinner? He is a psycho. I was seeing him for a few months and all was good. But then he smacked me around, so I pulled my .357 on him and haven't seen him since."

"He did what?" I growl down the phone. Zane puts out his cigarette and looks to me, stepping closer.

"He gave me a backhand, so I pulled my gun out of my bag and told him to fuck off and never come back. I haven't heard anything else from him since. Then I started seeing Treasure and suddenly I begin getting threats and random calls at different times of the day and night. I didn't want to tell you because well, you are you, and also I know what you guys would do."

"Fuck that, Phoebe! You should have fucking told me. Are you fucking shitting me? *Fuuuccckkk!*"

"Blake pl—"

She doesn't get to finish that sentence because I'm throwing my phone in front of me, feeling nothing but rage.

"B, what did she say?" Zane looks at me, not from a president's perspective, but from one best friend to another.

"He fucking hit her. She pulled her Gat on him and told him to never come back. Which he did until he found out about Treasure, then he started stalking and sending her death threats." I see

Zane's jaw clenching together. He used to change Phoebe's diapers when she was a baby, there's no way he's good with this.

"What the fuck is she thinking, getting involved with this shit? It's exactly why we set her up in New York to get her away from it all." He lights up another cigarette and I steal one from him. "He's done."

After finding out where Sinner was residing, we pull up to a grungy old flat. Wasting no time, I walk up to the door, kick it down and see two junkies shooting up needles on the sofa. Pulling my gun on them, they raise their hands up in defeat.

"Yo! What the fuck, man!"

"Where the fuck is Sinner?" They look between each other. "Now's not the fucking time to play games. If you want to live, you *will* tell me where the *fuck* Sinner is!" They both stand and try to run out the back door. Swinging my gun to them, I shoot them both one at a time in the back of the leg. They scream out and fall to the ground, turning around so they are lying on their backs and clutching their legs in pain.

"Stop! He'll be back soon, he just went to the store." I stand up the one that seems the most talkative, and shoot the other one square in the head, marking the walls with his blood and brain matter. I drag the other one over to the kitchen table while he cries out for his worthless friend.

"Brother?" Zane, Ade, and Felix ask uneasily behind me.

"You good?" Zane asks.

"Yeah, I need to do this. No one fucking hurts her, Zane. We promised her when she was a baby." He nods his head, making his way to the body lying soulless on the floor.

"I know, brother. I got you." He looks over to Felix and Ade. "Go get something to wrap this piece of shit in."

They begin to clean up the bloody mess on the ground while we wait. "You better hope he comes back, or that little performance you just saw happen to your friend, that won't even scratch the surface of what I'll do to you. You'll be begging me to put you out of your misery." He swallows while I stick duct tape across his mouth, forcing his mouth closed. I sit back in my chair and feel my phone vibrate in my pocket. It's a text message from Vicky, so I unlock my phone.

Vicky: *Did I do something wrong?*
Me: *Forget it and get some sleep.*
Vicky: *It's 7 pm…no one goes to sleep at 7 pm.*

Me: *Grandmas do. Sleep.*
Vicky: *I thought you might be different. I was wrong.*

I don't text her back. I have bigger fucking issues to deal with than her shit. I shove my phone back into my pocket, as I hear a car pull up and a door close. I hide behind one of the walls with Zane, Ade and Felix ahead of me. The door flies open, and when I know he's walked into the house enough, I come around the corner and pull him through into the kitchen covering his mouth in the process. I throw him into the wall until he gets back up, trying to fight me off. These idiots obviously know nothing about the Sinful Souls, we've been fighting since we could walk. The three of us anyway—me, Ade and Zane. I knock him in the jaw, which has him stumbling to the ground. Then get on top of his back, so I'm holding him down.

"If you so much as scream like the little bitch I know you are, I'll smash your face so far deep into this pavement your fucking teeth will be found in China. Are we understood?" I feel his head nod. Zane and Ade pull him up and sit him next to his junkie friend. I drag a seat up next to him, leaning in.

"Who the fuck do you think you are son?" He laughs, then spits to the ground. I take that as an *'I need to be a little more convincing,'* so I pull my knife out and stab his leg.

"You hit my sister, and then you shoot up my club?" Zane and I look at each other and laugh. "Got any last words?"

He laughs again. "Yeah, your sister likes it in the ass."

Instantly, after he's finished that sentence, I draw my knife out of his leg and stab it right into his temple. Circling it around, I make sure it effectively scrambles his brain. Once I know he's dead, I look over to the junkie, lift my gun and shoot him point blank in the head.

Now I feel satisfied.

"We need to tidy this shit up. Set it up right or Abby is going to have our ass on a platter," Zane says as I wipe the blood from my face. "I'm not done. Treasure is next."

VICKY

After getting no reply from Blake, I make my way to the kitchen and start pouring drink after drink. What a way to spend my last night here.

Fucking Blake fucking Rendon. Fuck him, and his sexy ass pack of fucking bikers.

Dwelling on my thoughts with bourbon in my hand, I start to over-think everything. So I make my way upstairs to run myself a bath. When it's full right to the very top, I slide in with my bottle in hand. This is why I hate relationships. This is why I avoid them. I hate the *'what's he thinking, what's he doing'* side of things. It sucks and we are not even close to being in a relationship. Picking up my phone, I scroll through my contacts and see

Ryder's added his number. So according to my drunk mind, I text him.

Stupid, why do I do this.

Me: *Ryder? Can you Ryd-er hard and fast? 'Her' being me.*

I laugh at myself realizing I'm very drunk. Actually, borderline wasted.

Ryder: *I guess only your mouth would know. ;) Are you drinking?*

My mouth does know, and my mouth wants it again. Fuck Blake.

Me: *We could change that.*

I text him my address.

Ryder: *Be there soon.*

After reading that line, I shoot up out of the bath. Water splashes all over the floor as my body lifts so fast. Which apparently is hilarious because I'm laughing so hard that I slip over in the huge puddle, smashing the side of my eye on the bathtub. Which is apparently even funnier. Now I have blood dripping from my eyebrow and I'm sitting here naked. My hair is everywhere and after all that, I still have an un-spilt bottle of bourbon held firmly in my hand.

Now that takes skill.

I pull on my nightie the best way I can and make my way downstairs to try to find a first aid kit. When I'm passing my front door, I hear a knock. So instead, I make my way to the door, opening it ready to greet Ryder. Only now I notice that it's Blake. My face drops, along with his.

"What the fuck happened to your eye?" I giggle while I tell him the story, slurring all over the place.

Oh wow! You really need to eat something, Vick.

He walks in shutting the door behind him and snatches the bottle out of my hand.

"What the fuck do you think you're doing?"

"What? I'm getting drunk. This is officially my last night here. I want to end it…drunk," I respond, snatching my bottle back off him while he's distracted in his thoughts.

"Like fuck. Unless you want to spend the night spewing, you need to put this shit down." He takes it away me and places it on the bench. I watch him eye me up and down and his face softens a little bit. At least I think it does. Then there's another knock at the door. My face pales, and I think I sober up a little at the realization of what's about to happen.

Stumbling to the door. *Okay, nope, definitely did not sober up at all.* I rush to answer it, but Blake beats me there.

"Easy tiger, go and sit down."

"No Blake, fuck—"

He opens the door, with Ryder standing on the other side.

BLAKE

"Ryder? What the fuck are you doing here?"

"Shit! Sorry, bro."

What the fuck. I look back at a very drunk Vicky, and her face is scrunched up like a kid that just got caught with her hand in the cookie jar.

"Care to explain?" I ask her, clenching my fists together.

She exhales quickly. "I texted Ryder to come over."

She fucking what?

"Fuck's sake, Vicky. I'm fucking over this shit." I look over to Ryder, who like always, thinks this is amusing.

"Blake, you fucking said that we could see other people," she slurs.

"Not fucking Ryder, not people I fucking know Vicky!"

She pauses, thinking it over for a second. "Shit! I didn't think of that. I'm sorry Blake."

Fuck, this girl is doing it all wrong. I look over to Ryder and say, "Leave."

He nods his head before getting back into his car and leaving. Shutting the door, I turn to her and see she still has blood running down her face.

"Come on, I'll clean you up."

She follows me to the kitchen. Lifting her up onto the bench, I start cleaning her cut with a disinfectant wipe. I'm trying really fucking hard not to look deep into her hazel eyes, but it's hard when the cut is right above them.

The way she looks at me? It's as if I'm the only man she sees.

I know that's not true because she just hit Ryder up less than an hour ago.

"Blake? I really do suck at all this. I don't know what to do." I fail and look into her eyes anyway.

"I know baby, me too. All I know is this. I don't want a relationship...ever. If you can live with that, then we can continue this. If you can't, then we need to stop now."

She pauses briefly. "No, I can do this. It's what I know. When are you coming back to Westbeach?"

"This weekend. Got a few loose ends to tie up here before we head back."

After leaving Sinner's, we made our way to see Tick, and to see what he knew about Treasure. It turned out he'd not been as forthcoming as we thought either. So he had us all chasing him down.

What the fuck is wrong with my sister and her choice in men? I do *not* fucking know.

Making our way into the living room, I pull Vicky down onto the sofa and turn the television on.

She shoots up out of nowhere and says, "I want ice cream!" Fuck, this girl is full time when she's drunk. She's like a little *Energizer Bunny.* I roll my hands over in a hurry up motion, making her quickly shoot up off the sofa. When she gets back, I see her with ice cream in one hand, and the bottle of Jack in the other. I go to reach for it, but she pulls back.

"Tsk tsk, biker. This is my last night and I *will* be spending it with my best mate Jack." I roll my eyes and pull her back down to the sofa.

"Can I ask you a question?" she says, looking up at me from under my arm.

"Yeah, shoot," I say looking back, trying to ignore the flood of feelings I'm getting just by staring at her.

She yawns and closes her eyes, almost whispering out her question, "Please don't have sex with anyone else," as she drifts off to sleep.

I'm almost certain she didn't mean to say that out loud, and the thought of even going near another woman makes my dick shrivel up anyway. Again, I'm left wondering why my lines get blurred with her.

VICKY

I wake to find myself ass up on the sofa, with ice cream all over my face and an empty bottle of Jack in front of me.

All class Abrahams. Mom would be proud.

Massaging my temples, I look over to see Blake asleep next to me. Lucky our sofa is big enough to sit ten people. Smiling, I make my way into the kitchen until I hear the doorbell ring.

"Fuck," I stutter out. Making my way to the annoying sound, I pull open the door to find Kalie on the other side looking just as bad me.

No strike that, maybe not as bad.

"You look like shit," I say to her.

"Likewise." She comes in, pushing me out of the way and walking into the kitchen. I sit down on the stool while she pours us a coffee.

"Blake's asleep, try not to be loud." She pauses and smiles at me.

I hear a deep scruffy voice come in through the door. "No, he's not. He just got woken up." Walking into the kitchen, he lays a kiss on my head. "Just going to jump in the shower." I nod my head while Kalie and I watch as he makes his way upstairs.

"Oh damn," Kalie purrs while licking her lips, making me burst out laughing.

"Miss Virgin got her cherry popped. Now all of a sudden she wants more?"

She laughs while taking a drink of her coffee. "Quite the opposite."

"Have you seen Ade?" I ask, getting some cereal out of the cupboard.

She shakes her head. "Nope, it was just a one-time thing. I couldn't have picked a better person to lose it to, though."

I scoff around a spoon of granola. "I could. He is a *biker,* Kalie. You're so not cut out for their shit."

"That...you are right about." We clink glasses and finish our coffee. After rinsing out our mugs, she comes over and gives me a big bear hug.

"Give my love to Alaina, would you?"

I squeeze her back. "I will. Make sure you visit soon, I'm going to miss you."

She wipes the tears off her cheek. "I'll miss you too, Vick."

Once she's left, I look up to the stairs and see Blake looking down at me.

"Who's Alaina?"

"Alaina is my BFF and my roomie. You may or may not get to meet her." He walks up to me, kissing me hard on the lips before picking me up.

"I have a few ideas of what we could do before you leave," he says, smiling against my lips.

"Oh, yeah? Please, do continue," I reply as he carries me to my room, kicking my door shut behind him.

BLAKE

I put her down and pull her face up to mine. "God, you're beautiful."

She tilts her head slightly, a light blush sweeping across her face. "Thank you. You're not too bad yourself." I smile at her, dragging my thumb across her lips while searching her eyes for some clue, any clue, that will tell me that doing this with her is a bad idea. But looking into her pleading eyes all I feel is want. I want this with her, more than anything. But I don't know how to do all this, and I know I'll fuck up. It's best for us to keep it casual, at least for now.

I lightly brush my lips over hers, and feel her breath hitch in her mouth and I smile. I grasp her hands in mine and pull them up behind my neck not usually liking this gesture. It fucking annoys me when chicks think they can touch you affectionately, the only thing they should be touching affectionately is my cock. Not Vicky though. Vicky is different, in so many different ways that she blows my fucking mind. And I know, I just know, that if I let her in her love will consume me. Own me, body and soul.

Kissing her deeply, I want to put all my fears into that one kiss. I don't want to not see her. She's been more than a fling, and right now, I don't want to fight it. She moans into my mouth. I slowly peel her clothes off, and then take off my cut and my T-shirt. She stops and looks up to me, I can see she wants to say something, so I smash my lips down on hers before something's said and this gets ruined. I pick her up, wrapping her legs around me and lay her down on the bed. Pulling my jeans off I come over the top of her, searching her eyes. She hooks her hands around my neck and brushes her nose against mine.

"This isn't goodbye, right? I'm going to see you when you get back? Tell me I'm going to see you when you get back," she asks, nervously looking into my eyes.

I smile at her. "You'll see me when I get back, baby. I promise." I kiss her all over her neck, bringing my hand down to her thigh and propping it up on my hip, sinking into her in one hard thrust. Pushing into her at a slow pace, savoring every moment of how good she feels wrapped around me. Thrusting harder and deeper, I circle her g-spot every time. Sweat is dripping off both of us as the slaps from both our bodies joining fills the air.

I bring my face down to her ear, "Come, baby, I want your pussy pulsing around my cock." And with that she releases around me, sucking me into her with every pulse. After filling her with my release, I roll off her and pull her under my arm, laying kisses on her head.

"I think…I'm going to miss you." She smiles.

I grunt and clear my throat. "Ditto, baby."

CHAPTER 8

Closing Vicky's door after seeing her off has me feeling fucked up—again. The lines that I set are almost non-existent. I get on my bike and head back to the hotel, eager to find this little fuckhead Treasure. Walking into my room, I pull my phone out to call Zane.

"Any update on Treasure?" I ask needing words with this peasant so I can get the fuck back to Westbeach.

"Yeah brother, got an address."

After giving me the details, I hang up the phone and ride out to see him, with Zane and Ade behind me. We pull up to a house—a basic house. But seeing his bike outside, we must be at the right place. Once we reach the front door, I knock a few times before kicking the door down, walking straight into the house with no weapon drawn. I could not give a fuck about a weapon; my fists can do just as much damage. We find Treasure in the shower. Pulling open the curtain, revealing him midway jacking off and it makes us all laugh aloud.

"What the fuck are you doing?" he yells, trying to grab hold of the curtain to cover himself, like the little bitch that he is. I pull the curtain away just in time so he misses it, making Zane and Ade laugh even harder. I squeeze my hand around the back of his neck, pulling him out of the shower and throwing him to the floor.

"What the fuck do you want with my sister?" I ask, with not a hint of humor in my voice.

He laughs, wiping the water out of his eyes. "She's a little slut. I never wanted her. She was the one all over *my* dick."

I kneel down so I'm at his level and chuckle. "Do you really think that I won't kill you? I can kill you without thinking twice," I say, smirking at him. I see his face drop, as he realizes the size of his cockiness, which is a lot bigger than his actual cock.

"You wouldn't. For what? What would be the purpose of killing me?" I shrug before pulling my knife out of its socket and stabbing him right in the dick. He screams out a blood-curdling scream that fucking irritates my ears, so I pull the knife out of his groin and slam it right between his eyes. Once I know he's out cold, I pull it out and spit on his face. *Fucking peasant.* My sister means the world to me, so make no mistake when I say that if anyone so much as breathes on her in a threatening way, I will fucking end them. Standing back up, I reach over to the bathroom sink and wash away the evidence of yet another life I've taken with this knife. I spare a glance in the mirror, seeing Zane looking at me.

"You good, brother?" he asks with eyebrows raised.

"Yeah, much better now."

"All right then, let's get this cleaned up."

It takes us a few hours to clean up the mess, but in the end, it will look like a drug do-over. Lucky for us, Treasure was also dealing crack from his house.

Fuck, my sister sure knows how to pick them. I need to have words with this girl next time I see her.

Arriving back to my hotel room, I slump down on my bed with my hands holding my face. Usually after the rough days, I get laid and fuck until I'm done. I want to. However, there's no one I want under me other than Victoria fucking Abrahams.

Well, I'll be damned.

Sighing out loud and scrubbing my face in frustration, I pick up my phone and a text comes through as I'm holding onto it. That fucking text makes me one happy man. And at this very moment, I know that tonight I'm dragging all the boys back home just so I can see that earth-shattering fucking smile.

VICKY

The drive home is longer than the drive there. I cannot wait to see Alaina, but at the same time I miss Blake. Walking into our apartment, I drop all my bags into my room and start unpacking. Blake is constantly on my mind. I wish I could erase feelings because feelings will get you killed. I pull out my phone and text message Blake.

Me: *Come see me when you are back?*
Blake: *I'll be back this weekend, babe. Will stop in on the way home.*
Me: *Okay :)*
Blake: *What are you wearing?*

Me: *I can wear whatever you want me to wear.*
Blake: *In that case, be wearing nothing.*
Me: *Your wish is my command.*

I fluff my hair up and put my phone on auto-timer. Sitting it on my chest of drawers, I kneel on my bed with my hands over my boobs and a broad smile on my face, pulling my lip in between my teeth, then I shoot the photo sending him evidence of what he wanted from me. After five minutes of no reply, I start to get nervous. Picking up my phone, I examine what I took. I'm scrutinizing myself, trying to find something wrong with the photo, but there's nothing that I can see. My phone finally receives a text and alerts me with a ding. Seeing his name splashing on my screen makes my stomach feel like it is doing backflips.

Blake: *Jesus fucking Christ woman. I'll be back tonight.*

I clap my hands in glee—that got the required response. Even though I only saw him hours earlier, I need to see him again. I know I'm beginning to feel many different feelings for him, but at this point, I'm good with that. After I've unpacked all my crap, I send a text to Alaina, forgetting that I haven't seen her in three weeks, and we usually always have plans for the weekend.

> Me*: I cannot believe we have planned nothing to do this weekend…I'm getting an itchy liver, it needs alcohol.*
> Alaina: *It's Monday, we can plan tonight over tacos. But I'm worried about that itchy liver…The future doctor in me says that's a symptom of Primary Biliary Cirrhosis, but the best friend in me screams too much alcohol.*
> Me: *Do not cuss at me. Never, ever, too much alcohol. You can diagnose me over tequila shots this weekend at The Point. We can start our weekend shenanigans there.*
> Alaina: *Sounds like a plan.*

I love Alaina like a sister. We have been best friends since we were eight and have been inseparable since. Picking up my handbag, I make my way down our dorm and out to the car park, ready to buy some bits and pieces for dinner tonight. Getting into my car my phone dings again. I get all excited thinking it's Blake, but only to look down and see Jesse's name. *Fuck.*

> Jesse: *Hey Vick, are you back?*

At this point, I don't want to reply. Jesse and I were close. He was the missing piece to Alaina and me, and although she always told me not to sleep with friends, I didn't listen. I wish I did because now it's all sorts of complicated. He doesn't make it easier on me, either.

Me: *Hey, yeah I am.*
Jesse: *Can we talk?*

I laugh. There's definitely nothing I have left to say to him. He took our so-called *'relationship'* too far and he knows it.

Me: *There's nothing left to say, Jesse. Could we just leave it now?*

I slide my phone back into my bag before I see another message from him. Then I'll have to open it and lose my shit on him, so instead I set off to the store. Westbeach is, I guess, a small town. All beaches and sun and I love it. My parents were raised here and so was I. But when my dad decided to leave my mother for a girl I went to school with, my mom moved to Paris to live the extravagant—as she would put it—widow lifestyle. I love my mom. She's my rock and even though she's not around much, I know she'll always be there for me.

My dad is too, but I still haven't decided whether I trust him again. Once you've seen your mom betrayed by the one man that was not supposed to let her down, your opinion of him changes. Well, mine did.

I'm pulling all my grocery bags out of the boot ready to take inside when Jesse runs up behind me.

Fuck. My. Motherfucking life.

"Vicky, can we talk?" he asks, coming straight into my personal bubble. I really wish he would just leave it alone.

"What do you want to say, Jesse?"

He takes one of the bags from me. "I made a mistake, I'm sorry. Can we just be friends?" I shut the boot and turn to him.

"Friends? And you will be okay with that?"

He looks around unsure, so I roll my eyes and make my way inside. I already know he's not all right with it.

"Just give me some time, Vick. Please. Fuck!"

I keep walking as he runs up behind me. I love Jesse like a friend, but I really wish we never went there. Now the mere thought of having sex with him makes me feel sick to my stomach. I'm still scowling when we burst through the door, and I'm double stepping in hopes that I might leave him behind.

"Hey guys, couldn't wait for you sorry. I needed a wine," Alaina says as I put all the shopping bags onto the bench.

"I'm going to need more than wine to get me through this shit," I mumble under my breath.

"Have a good day?" Alaina asks, looking at me with her eyes wide and happy. I know she's just trying to put me in a good mood.

"Just perfect," I reply sarcastically. Jesse has set me off in a bad mood. I just want Blake, he's all I want right now and being around Jesse makes me miss him even more.

I start straight away making tacos. I love cooking. Pour me a good glass of wine with great music, and you'll not see me for hours.

Who am I kidding? It doesn't even have to be a good glass of wine, but it definitely has to be good music.

I give Jesse the lettuce and tell him to chop it up. He looks at me with his puppy eyes and for a second, I'm reminded as to why I was attracted to him in the first place. He's the all-American boy, harmless looking with ocean blue eyes. He's safe, and what I should be attracted to.

Unfortunately, my body is a fussy bitch that prefers bad boys with tattoos. Ones that ride Harleys, and have secret clubs where you can have hot group orgies.

"I'm sorry, Vick. Give me some time?" he asks, looking at me with pleading eyes. I soften toward him.

"Okay, I'll try." I smile briefly at him. I want to try, if not for us then for Alaina because she loves the shit out of this kid.

Once I've made up our plates we go and join Alaina on the sofa, sinking our teeth into the fatty goodness. My next favorite thing to do—under having sex with Blake. I take a large drink of my wine.

"So, I met someone during the holidays." I decide to spit out in the spur of the moment because I fucking miss him. I'm also hoping it will help move Jesse along too.

"What?" Alaina asks, taking a huge mouthful of her drink.

"I don't know, I guess it's not serious. That's why I hadn't told you earlier." I smile at her. God, there's so much I want to tell this girl.

"Well, spill woman. I'm not going to wait forever!"

"Not much to spill really. His name is Blake. He's sexy, funny and all things nice, but he also comes with a crazy ex-girlfriend, fucked up past, and commitment issues. He's made it clear we can't be anything more, I'll just have to live with it," I tell her leaving out the fact that he owns a swingers bar, and that I had two different threesomes with him while I was away.

"What the fuck?" Jesse spits, with anger written all over his face.

"Jesse, calm down. What we had wasn't serious and you knew that," I say, rolling my eyes at his outburst.

"Well, all right. Aside from this little blast that I've heard now, which by the way, I expect to hear more about." Alaina points at us both. "When can I meet him?" I look over at her, taking another drink of my beverage.

"This weekend—I think. He's part of the Sinful Souls Motorcycle Club, they'll be back this weekend."

Jesse scoffs. "Oh, real classy Vicky."

I turn my attention, ready to rip into him. "Shut up, Jesse. You don't know shit."

He laughs while taking another drink. "I don't know shit? You don't know shit, Vicky. You're fucking blind! You can't see a good thing when it's sitting right in front of your face."

Throwing my head back, I laugh. "What, you're the...*good thing*? No, Jesse. Never." He shakes his head angrily.

"I can't wait to meet him," Alaina confirms, bringing my attention back to her.

"I'm going to go. Thanks for the invite, Lain," Jesse replies, making his way out the door.

Fucking dramatic.

"Oh Jesse, don't be like that—" Alaina says a little too late because he slams the door on his way out effectively cutting her off. She looks over to me, with one of her perfectly arched eyebrows raised.

"You couldn't tell him before? Instead of spilling it out in the open like that?" I pick up my plate and make my way to the sink. I'm so over this day, and so ready to see my sexy biker man even though he's not actually mine.

A girl can dream, can't she?

"No, he needs to get it, Lain. I told him, *just casual*, but like a grade-A-clinger, he got too attached." She picks up her plate and we walk out to do the dishes.

"In his defense, though, I've heard you between these walls and I don't blame him." I laugh and whip her on the ass with the tea towel.

"Shut up!" I pause for a second. "I don't think I'll be able to make it out this weekend, I'll see how I go."

"Because your mysterious man is coming?" she asks, wiggling her eyebrows.

"Precisely. He's just...oh man. And the men in his club? Oh my God. I wanted them all." She laughs, knowing what I'm like.

“How was Kalie?”

“She was good, but that’s a long story and I’m tired.” I wink at her, putting down the dishcloth. A few minutes later, we make our way to bed.

After my shower, I fire up my laptop and begin on some early preparations for tomorrow. Who would pick political science? Oh wait, I did. I'm two hours into my study when I get a text message. I pick up my phone and see Blake's name across the screen, setting off a million butterflies in my tummy.

Blake: *Almost there, babe.*

A rush of emotions start pulling at me as the idea sinks in that I'm going to see him any minute.

Me: *I'll meet you outside. It's too hard to explain how to get here.*

Pulling on my yoga pants with my WBC T-shirt, I make my way downstairs while putting my hair into a high ponytail. I hear the bikes before I see them, I swear that sound is like music to my clit. The sound cuts off when I reach the doors. Pushing them open, I see Blake sitting on his bike, pulling off his helmet with a broad smile resting on his lips. I run straight into his arms. Jumping on him, wrapping my legs around his waist and kissing him like I haven't seen him in a century.

"Hey baby," he says, his deep voice pulling all sorts of strings deep in my soul.

"Hey. How was your trip?" I ask, stepping back so he can actually get off his bike.

Me and my damn impulsive actions.

I think for a second that maybe I took that too far.

"Long, because all I wanted to do was see you," he replies, pulling me back to him, grabbing my ass.

Mmm, this is exactly where I want to be.

I watch Zane roll his eyes. "Come on, Romeo and Juliet. You coming or not?" he asks, looking right at me, obviously wanting to get out of here.

He's scary when he's serious.

"I can't, I've got so much to sort out for tomorrow."

Did I mention that being a student sucks?

I look up to Blake and see he's clenching his jaw. I bring my hand up, running it over his jawline and down his neck. I'm waiting for him to pull away from me, but he doesn't. That thought alone makes my insides jump up and down.

"Do you guys want to come up?" I ask, looking into Blake's eyes, which I haven't been able to do very often because they're filled with so much raw, complicated emotion that it knocks me on my ass.

"Yeah babe, we can do that." He smiles down at me, running the back of his hand across my cheek. My face pushes up against his touch instantly. It's a sweet gesture that leaves me feeling a little confused. Before I can explore those feelings, the front doors slam open again, revealing my half-asleep best friend. I giggle because she looks cute.

"Lain? What are you doing?" I ask, looking over at her lazily. Blake does crazy things to me.

"Me? I woke to find *you* not in your bed. So I went to try and find you."

I laugh and point to Blake. "This is Blake."

"Hi, I'm Alaina." She looks unsure. Alaina is different, and innocent in a way I guess, I have always felt the intense need to protect her like a little sister.

"Blake," he replies, smirking at her. I roll my eyes because I know he's checking her out—it's hard not to. For one, she's from New Zealand, which gives her an exotic, different feel about her. And two, she's incredibly sexy.

"What's that accent I can pick up there?" Blake asks.

"A Kiwi accent, I'm from New Zealand." I can see Blake about to say something else, so I shoot him a glare. Alaina has not had the easiest life. She moved to Westbeach when she was eight. Being shy and hardly speaking, a few girls tried to pick on her until I put them back into their place. Since day one I've taken her under my wing. I love her to bits. Blake must see the look in my eyes, so he changes what he was about to say.

"Well, okay, little Kiwi. This is my brother, Zane." I look over to Alaina and see the blush that reveals itself cross over her face. I smile because I know that look. Not on her, because she hasn't actually had a boyfriend long enough to judge that by, but I know *that* look.

This should be interesting.

"Zane," he replies, and for the first time since I've met Zane Mathews, he looks interested in something. The same could be said about Alaina, she's always kept her head in her books and I've always respected her for it. She's strong, don't get me wrong. The girl can hold her own, so I'm not worried about her and Zane as much as I was about Ade and Kalie.

"All right, nice meeting you guys. Vick? I'll see you inside?" I look at her and then gaze over to Blake.

"They're going to come up. Is that okay? It'll just be for a little bit, I promise?" She shoots me more evil glares, and I *think* she just might kill me for this.

Walking back inside, I jump onto Blake, wrapping my arms around him. He laughs, walking off to my room leaving Alaina with Zane.

Oh please, she will be thanking me, I'm sure.

When we arrive at my room, he places me down on my bed softly.

"Fuck," he mumbles under his breath while looking deep into my eyes. I cock my head sideways, looking between his eyes and his lips.

"What? What's wrong?" I ask, smiling down at him.

God, he's beautiful. The perfect amount of bad boy mixed with the perfect amount of beautiful.

"Nothing, I think…" He presses his lips softly against mine, with no tongue. He just kisses me. Getting in-between my legs, he pulls me to him putting pressure on the place that's absolutely throbbing for his touch. I can't help a little moan that escapes my mouth. I fucking missed this man so much. It almost hurt to be away from him. He pulls away and looks at me, searching for something in my eyes.

"What are you doing to me, Vicky?" I rest my face on his hand, placing a kiss on his fingers.

"I'm sure that the feeling is mutual."

He takes his hand away and wraps it around the back of my neck, pulling my face to his so our foreheads are touching.

"You know we can't *actually* be together, right? Your lines are still where they should be?" Fighting the urge not to scowl at his comment, I nod my head.

"My lines will be fine," I reply. Then he kisses me, using his lips to push me over onto my back while he comes up to me putting both his fists on either side of my head. He looks at me for a while, and God, I wish I knew what was going on behind those eyes. By the look on his face, it seems as though he's fighting an internal battle. Then his eyes turn soft as a slow smile spreads across his lips.

Reaching down, he brushes my hair out of my face and kisses me again, this time taking my left thigh in his hand and pulling it open so he's lying right against my middle.

Would it be entirely inappropriate to just rub myself against him until I come?

Yes, yes Vicky, it would. Instead, I start to pull his T-shirt and cut off him, throwing them onto the ground.

Holy fuck, this man takes my breath away.

He reaches down and slides my T-shirt off before getting up to pull my pants down. I arch off the bed to give him easier access. Feeling so sensitive right now, I think if he touched me where I want to be touched, I might just explode. My breathing becomes needy as he slowly slides his hands over my body, tormenting me. Looking up to him, I find a cocky smirk on display all over his face.

"This. Is. Mine. For the night." My belly flips at the beginning of his sentence, only to be shut down by the end part.

Why can't I be yours forever?

Hooking his finger under my panties, he pulls them down in one swift move, leaving me naked on the bed. He drags my panties up to his nose, smelling them briefly before smiling down at me with nothing but lust on his face.

Why did that just turn me on?

Unbuckling his buckle, he pulls his jeans down letting his cock spring free. I look at it with hunger on my face.

God, I just want to ravish this man.

Moving back on top of me, he lays me down flat on my back, kissing me while beginning to make his way down south. My toes curl and my eyes roll back as he lightly runs his tongue on the outside of my cleft, while still running little kisses on that spot where my thighs meet my middle. By this point, I'm panting like a sex driven maniac, because that's what he does to me. When he finally licks one light lick right over my clit, I scream out in pleasure.

He begins his slow, torturous pace, making love to my pussy with his mouth and after a few minutes my orgasm slams into me at full force, making my body shudder in euphoria. He comes back up to me with a cocky smile on his face.

"That was fucking hot. Come here, baby." This man is going to be the death of me. He begins to lick from my collarbone up to my ear, as he's doing that he pushes into me. I throw my head back, getting lost in the feeling of his thick, large cock filling me. He's putting pressure on my g-spot with every thrust. I place my hands on his neck, but he pulls them back down wrapping them together and putting them over my head.

Are we really doing the several shades of fucked up thing again? I don't think much into it because I'm too busy lost in the feeling of this hot as fuck man rubbing his dick flush up against my pleasure spot, there's no better feeling in the world. I'm completely obsessed with having sex with him.

He begins slowly pushing in and pulling out of me. I look up to him making eye contact and the look he's giving me right at this very moment has me feeling like maybe his lines are becoming just as confused as mine. Then I remind myself that this is just sex, this man is sexing me, not making love to me. A few deep thrusts later and I'm coming all over again, seeing stars.

Holy fuck Vicky, pull your sex in line.

I kiss him while riding out my orgasm. Slowly I push at him, making the impression that I want to be on top. He rolls over onto his back while I straddle him. He laughs, looking up at me.

"What? Is this you trying to take back control baby?" I slowly smirk at his comment.

"You will never know sweetheart," I say, quoting his comment from Sinsation. He laughs again before pulling my face down to his, and we kiss for what feels like ages. The kisses feel intimate too, or maybe that's just my female brain over thinking the situation. He makes his way down to my breasts. Putting one in his mouth, he licks my nipple then moves to the other while looking up at me.

Holy fuck.

I start to ride on his dick slowly as he lays back down, putting his hands on my hips. I pick up my pace, and when he moans I swear to God it's the sexiest thing I've ever heard. I ride him hard, both of us dripping in sweat until we reach our climax. Feeling his dick twitch inside me, I flop down onto him, catching my breath.

"Holy fuck," I say against his chest. I feel his hands wrap around my body before he lays a kiss on my head.

"I know." And with that simple reply, he gives me a hint of hope.

"Are you going to stay the night?" I ask, climbing off him and realizing we didn't wear a condom *again*. It's a good thing I'm on the pill, but the fact that he didn't ask should worry me, though. He gets up and throws his jeans on.

"Not tonight, babe," he says while he pulls on his clothes. My face drops a little but when he notices he comes over to me, hooking a finger under my chin and tilting it up to face him. "Don't pout, I'll see you tomorrow." I drop my lip, giving him puppy eyes and he laughs while throwing his head back, making me smile. "You're fucking sexy cute. You know that," he says.

I stand up to wrap my arms around him. "Then why won't you stay with me?"

He brings my hands back down, kissing them gently. “Because Vicky…because you deserve better than me.”

He kisses me one last time, then walks out the door, leaving me there speechless. What the fuck does he mean, “I deserve better than him”? The man is giving me whiplash with his mood swings.

Nice Vicky, just go and quote Twilight why don’t you, I think while mentally facepalming myself.

Deciding I’m over this long ass day, I get back into bed and close my eyes. I’m aware and shitty at the fact that I’ll be starting back at school in less than ten hours.

Great!

I wake up so early that it's still dark outside. "Fuck." Turning over, I pick up my phone and see that is 4:08 in the morning and groan because there's no way I'll be able to get back to sleep now. I sit up in my bed just looking at my phone. Pulling out my headphones, I turn on Metallica's *'The Unforgiven'* while I try to forget my growing feelings for this completely complicated man. After five minutes, I decide I can't sit still and I need to text him.

Me: *I don't know if I can do this.*

Dropping my phone back down, I listen intently to the music playing in my ears. Getting up, I make my way into the living room to watch some crappy early morning television and not long after I sit down, there's a knock on my door. Turning the television onto mute, I get up to answer it. I pull the door open to Blake standing there leaning up against the doorframe with his hands in his pockets all freshly showered in jeans, a black T-shirt showing his defined muscles, his cut and black combat boots.

"Hey," I say shyly because I'm not expecting him to show up on my damn doorstep.

"What do you mean you *'don't know if you can do this'*?" He looks at me with his mouth set in a straight line.

"Come in," I say, waving toward the inside of my apartment. He walks in and sits on the sofa, spreading his legs out.

"Do you want a drink or anything?" I ask him as I move to the kitchen to turn the light off. Now the only light we have is coming directly from the television.

"I don't want anything to drink, Vicky. Tell me what you meant?" I sit on the opposite side of the sofa, not intentionally it just happened to be where my body took me.

"I...I don't know. I'm getting confused with the feelings I'm beginning to have for you." He clenches his fists together on top of his knee while looking up to me.

I swear this man looks sexy in whatever face he pulls.

"Zane will be here soon, don't ask because I don't know."

Interesting, if I weren't so caught up in our shit I'd ask why. He throws his arms over the edge of the sofa, looking over at me and a slow smile comes to his lips.

"I won't bite…*hard*." He pats the spot next to him before biting his bottom lip.

What the fuck. This man was born to turn women on. It's not fair.

I move next to him, without touching, until he pulls me on top of him so I'm spread across his legs. He puts his face in the crook of my neck.

"Don't think too much into this Vicky, or it will fuck with you. But for the moment know this, I can't think of anyone past you. You've put up this invisible wall in front of every other girl. I see *no one,* and I want *no one* else on my dick but you."

I smile at him, and then he kisses me on the lips. How the fuck can I *not* think too much into that comment, when he just said the sweetest thing I'll probably ever hear come out of his mouth? "I'll try not to."

He smiles a small smile. I wonder how his crazy ex-girlfriend managed to crack his wall down.

Maybe we should exchange advice. She can tell me how to pull Blake's wall down, and I'll tell her how to not be such a disgusting slutbag.

Rolling off him, I get up and just as I stand. H grabs my arm pulling me back down to him. He pushes my lips to his, giving me a quick kiss.

"Feel like a big breakfast?" I ask as I get back up, looking down on him.

"Always," he responds, slapping my ass as I walk to the kitchen. Just when I get started on breakfast, I hear a knock on the door.

"Blake? It'll be Zane," I yell out from the kitchen.

I don't really know Zane at all, and I know I've not seen him with any other women. But I wouldn't be a friend if I didn't remind him of *exactly* what will happen if he hurts my best friend. Turning on my Bose sound dock, I turn up Snoop Dogg's *'Wiggle'* while I get started on making breakfast. Looking over to the living room every few seconds I see the boys deep in conversation. Putting the bacon in the pan, I turn around to find Alaina standing in the living room, staring holes into my head.

"The fuck Vick, turn it down!" she moans, covering her ears.

I turn to her laughing, "No can do, sugar. I'm on a good vibe this morning. All I want to do is dance."

I drop it low and start shaking my ass in front of her grumpy face.

"You know I love you and all that, but if you don't turn it down now, I just might cut you in your sleep." I laugh as she walks back into her room, and a few seconds later, Zane follows her in.

There it is.

I dish out our plates, taking them into the living room and sitting down next to Blake as I bite into the streaky bacon. Blake looks at me in amusement.

"How is it that you can eat all this, but never show for it?"

I lick the fatty goodness off my finger, taking it deep into my throat. "Good genes?"

He drops his food back onto his plate and squeezes under my chin with one hand, pulling my face into a kiss. He skims over my bottom lip with his thumb, pulling it into his mouth and sucking the bacon taste from it. "Don't ever do that sexy shit again, not in public." Then he smiles while pulling his finger out of his mouth.

How can that turn me on so much?

"You know…" I was just about to say something until I hear moaning come from Lainy's room. "What the fuck?" I whisper to Blake. He shrugs his shoulders and chuckles.

"Don't know what's going on there, but Zane doesn't usually sleep with the first girl he sees."

I take a bite out of my waffle. "Is he a—"

Blake cuts me off, shaking his head. "Don't do the *murderer* thing again. Unless you want the truth?" he asks with an arched eyebrow. I think over what he's just asked, *would I want to know? Do I already know?* I shrug, carrying on with my food.

"Maybe one day. Not today, though."

After taking my plate to the sink, I make my way down to my room just in time to see Zane, who's walking out of Alaina's room with perfect *'just fucked'* hair. I decide that now is a good time to throw a little warning into the air.

"If you hurt her—" I begin to say to him before he cuts me off.

"You will do nothing because you can't. And what I do with her is none of your business."

Cocky son of a bitch.

I raise my eyebrows and cock my head back. "Like fuck I'll be settling for that as an answer," I say, spinning around as he carries on out the door. I notice he's not going to stop his speedy exit.

"Just remember one thing, *Zane*..." I pause momentarily. "You're not the only one who sleeps with a nine under their pillow." He stops briefly, turns and throws me a smirk before carrying on out the front door. I make my way over to Blake, seeing an impressed look on his face. "Don't go there, Blake."

He laughs while shaking his head. "I wasn't going to say anything."

A couple hours later, I decide to go in and see Alaina. Walking to her room, I swing the door open.

Feeling a little theatrical, are we?

"Speak...now," I say after seeing her sitting up in her bed with a huge smile on her face.

"I'm pretty sure I don't need to tell you anything, I think you heard it all this morning." She gets up and walks to the bathroom, so I follow.

"Yes, I did. I don't know, Lain. I don't know if this is a good idea. And Blake says he's the *'tap and gap'* kind of man, not the *'clean you up and lay your head down'* type." Saying that, was probably a low blow but as always, my intense need to protect this girl comes in at full speed.

"Vicky, calm down. We were both tired is all."

Yeah, I'm sure you were both exhausted, I say sarcastically in my head.

She continues, "It won't happen again. I've got to keep my head in my studies."

I laugh while walking out the door. “Lain, you can study and still get fucked at the same time,” I respond, being my crass self. Leaving her sitting there, beet-red.

After class, I text Blake to see what he’s doing for the rest of the day. It’s as if we have an unspoken wall up between us. A wall that says, *‘You can’t be with me, but you’re not allowed to be with anyone else either.’* I think many people can relate to that wall, at least once in their life.

Me: *Are you busy?*
Blake: *Heading home now.*
Me: *Want to meet at Billy Joes?*
Blake: *Yeah, I’ll meet you there.*

After getting into some skinny jeans and a vest, I get into my car and make my way to Billy Joe’s, thinking about my growing feelings for him. I smile as memories come flashing back of all our times together. I never thought that I’d ever meet a man that I could actually see myself settling down with, but Blake changes all of that.

Walking in, I see him sitting at the bar drinking. When he sees me, he gives me a sexy smile, setting off butterflies again deep in my stomach.

There really is no coming back from this.

He gets up, pulling me in for a bear hug before I sit down on the chair next to him.

"How's your day been?" I ask him, ordering a glass of water because Alaina has told me that I really do need to settle down on the drinking.

"A little crazy. Nothing new," he responds, looking away from me. I don't know why, but I feel as though he's not telling me something.

"You okay? You look a little stressed?" He glances over at me, looking deep into my eyes.

"I need to tell you something. I didn't—" He's interrupted by the door swinging open loudly. I see Alaina standing in the doorway with fear smeared all over her face.

"Lain, babe, what's wrong?" I ask, standing from my seat and making my way over to her. I've never seen her *this* freaked out.

"Vick, a car's been following me. I saw it today on campus and then again just now while I was out on my run. It was following behind me, so I kept my normal pace hoping they didn't know I noticed them." I stop in my tracks and feel as though ice is running through my blood for a second.

"Do you think...do you think this has anything to do with your parents?" Alaina's parents disappeared when she was eight, which resulted in her coming to live in Westbeach. However, there's so much more to it. Alaina used to tell me about a man that said he wanted her when she was of age. I don't know what sort of activities her parents were into, but I certainly get the feeling it was dangerous.

"I don't know, maybe. Why now, though? Why after all these years will he be coming after me?" I look to Blake and see him looking around the room.

"I don't know. I don't understand why else I'd be getting followed." Blake gets up out of his seat, making his way outside before coming back in.

"Black Mercedes? Still there across the street. I'm going to call Zane." Alaina starts to shake her head in horror, and if we were under any other circumstances, I would laugh.

"No, please don't. I don't want to be that annoying girl after a one night stand."

"Babe, you'll never be *'that annoying girl after a one night stand.'* You need hooker heels for that," he assures her, smiling his cocky smile while he walks off dialing Zane.

"Vick, people are going to begin to find out about my past." I grab onto her hand. It's something we always do when one or the other is in distress.

"I know, it's going to be okay, though. You're not going anywhere."

I'll do everything and anything in my power to stop her from having to run. And if she does end up having to run, I'm going with her. There's no way I can live without this girl.

"Lain? It's going to be okay."

She shakes her head, bringing her fingers to her mouth. "No. No, it's really not, Vick. Zane…I feel things for him. Things I shouldn't and," she stops for a second to gather her thoughts, "he's never going to want anything to do with me when he finds out about all my shit."

I think she's wrong, I think Zane likes her just as much as she obviously likes him. Lucky for some, relationships can be black and white. Not mine, though. Oh no. Mine has all sorts of colors splashed in and mixed together, causing fucking pain to even look at. She starts pacing just as we hear a loud rumble of bikes shaking the walls of the bar. The door flies open and an outraged Zane strolls in. I notice the look he gives Alaina, and it's interesting to see such an emotionally shut off man have a soft spot for my friend.

After she explains everything to Zane, I notice the boys shuffle around on their feet. I glance over to Blake and he mouths, "Are you okay?"

Nodding my head in reply before going back to my seat and leaving them all to talking. I can't stop thinking about what Blake was about to tell me. I peer over to the crowd in front of me while I'm swallowing my drink when I hear a growl come from Zane.

"Drop it, Ade."

Oh dear, trouble in biker paradise?

"Pack your shit Alaina, you have two hours."

She glares an evil stare at him and says, "Snappy much?" before storming off.

Yep, I have nothing to worry about as far as Alaina goes. She's a natural with bossy dominant men, obviously.

Once Zane has left the building to follow her, I swing my chair back around to face the bar. "I'll get a sauv, please," I say to the old bartender.

So much for drying out.

The rest of the boys sit down at the bar as well, ordering drinks. Blake comes and sits down next to me.

"Come, I need to talk to you." He takes hold of my hand, taking me to a corner in the bar. I look over to the boys and see them looking directly at me knowingly. Harvey gives me a small smile and it looks like a smile of pity. Once we reach a booth, I look over to Blake and go to sit opposite him. Something's telling me this cannot be good.

"What are you doing? Come here," he says, pulling me over to where he is so I'm sitting across his lap.

"What is it, Blake? Just spit it out."

CHAPTER 11

One hundred thoughts are rushing through my mind. Does he have kids? Is he married? Does he lock people in his basement while performing sexual acts on them? You never know in this day and age what people are capable of, they are into some kinky shit.

"Before I say what I'm about to say, I want you to know something. I had no idea I was going to have these kinds of feelings for you. You came into my life at full speed, causing me to crash off my track that I've been driving for so long," he squeezes me into him before continuing, "I'm fucking sorry, Vicky." I look down at him from his lap.

"Are you married?"

He shakes his head.

Well, at least I don't have to kill him.

"Zane was asked to take Alaina into protection, so a few months ago we set up this plan." I swallow roughly, not wanting to look at him. "The plan was that I was to start seeing you in order to get to Alaina. I'm fucking sorry Vicky. The feelings for you, though—" I stand, pushing his hands away from me, beginning to walk backward as he walks toward me.

"You fucking *used* me? All of everything was a fucking *lie?"* I feel so embarrassed. How easy was I? I gladly and readily opened up to this man, thinking he was truly attracted to me.

"Vicky, stop! As I said before, the feelings I feel for you are very fucking *real*."

"Fucking stop, Blake! Your word means *nothing* to me now. You *lied, embarrassed me* and *shat* on me. Forget it, just leave me alone and don't contact me...*ever*."

I walk out of the bar trying not to cry. I've never cried over a man before, but as they say, there's a first time for everything. Getting into my car, the strong face that I kept on while walking out of there begins to crumble before my very eyes. A single sob escapes my mouth. Bringing my hands to my face, I let go. Every good feeling that this man made me feel has just been ripped away from me and replaced with hurt, deceit, and lies. I'm shattered. He obviously meant a hell of a lot more to me than I gave him credit for. I hear a knock on my window and look up to see him standing there.

"Open the fucking door, Vicky." He tries yanking my door open.

Great, now he's just seen you crying fucking tears over him.

He looks manic with his pupils dilated. Probably feeling a little guilty for what he's done to me, nothing more and nothing less. I can't even be angry at him about the way I feel toward him because he's always made it quite clear that we were never going to be anything more.

"Vicky, I fucking swear to fucking God, if you don't open this door now I'm going to smash your fucking window. Please baby, please don't cry."

I wipe the tears away from my eyes, start the car and floor it the fuck out of there. I know I'll never *ever* want anything to do with him after this.

BLAKE

"Fuck!" I yell as I see Vicky take off onto the highway. I fucking feel like shit. I should never have agreed to this fucking parade, she deserves so much better than what I could ever give her. As

much as I want to pursue her, *need* to pursue her, I won't do it. The girl means that much to me that I don't want to fucking damage her by just being with her. Walking back into the bar, I'm retracing the tracks in my mind trying to figure out the exact moment that I fell completely in love with Victoria Abrahams. *Fuck.* I stumble in, smashing the door open. I see the boys all staring at me.

"Don't! I just need a drink," I say to them, and Ade pulls out the chair next to him.

"So," Ade says, picking up his drink. I really hope he doesn't say anything smart. Ade is fucking lethal, but I'll gladly give him a go right now.

"Did you tell her you loved her?" he asks, peering at me over his glass. I drink mine in one hit before tapping the bench for another.

"Nope, there's no point. She deserves better." He turns to me with disbelief written on his face.

"That's some bullshit brother, and you know it."

I laugh. "You a relationship expert now? Mr. I-Have-Not-Had-One-Single-Girlfriend in all of my twenty-eight years?" He laughs while drinking the rest of his beer.

"Touché, brother."

Ade is complicated. He's the biggest out of all of us and the most ruthless, and that's saying something because the rest of us don't walk around with pussy pouches on. But Ade? He's on a whole different level of dangerous. He hasn't once had a girlfriend. He has his casuals, and he treats them as exactly what they are—garbage. But they always come back, they all want to save him, or attain the unattainable. No one has ever caught his attention, except for Kalie.

"What happened with Kalie?" I ask with a smirk. I haven't actually brought this up with him before, but I'm feeling reckless so why not. He flinches briefly, then smiles.

"Nothing, I did the deed and that was that." I laugh, looking back at him.

"Something tells me there's a lot more to it than that. When she left me she was all *'I still want my V card, but I will suck your dick, though.'* Gotta say, the chick was on a mission." Ade stands from his seat, looking at me with absolute disgust and murder in his eyes.

"She fucking *what?"* I laugh again and stand up in front of him. Ade is my brother, I grew up with him and Zane, we fight like brothers, but I love him nonetheless.

"She sucked my dick brother. She was balls deep in that shit while I was licking Vicky's sweet spot. She was fair—" The first fist flies into my face.

"You piece of fucking shit!" Harvey and Felix pull him off me from the floor and I laugh.

"She was fair fucking game, Ade. You were too busy with the slut spread out in front of you to care," I continue, spitting the blood out of my mouth onto the floor. He's breathing in and out at breakneck speed, so I get up and grab my drink. "Are you done?" I ask, watching his face calm and his eyes settle.

"Don't ever, fucking speak about her *ever* again. Understood?" he replies. I look at him and narrow my eyes. I know without him saying anything that she's different. I'm intrigued.

"She's different?" I ask with a knowing expression.

"Drop it, Blake. I fucking mean it."

Harvey looks at me and shakes his head. "Kalie is a touchy subject. Don't go there, brother. I tried." I nod my head in understanding before sitting back down to finish my beer.

"Are you seeing her now or what?" I ask. *No one tells me anything.* Or maybe I have been too caught up in my own shit. Between Vicky, my sister, and Zane's mission he has me on, I haven't been able to take a breather.

He shakes his head, setting his mouth into a hard line. "She was a one-night thing. I should never have done it. It's hard to turn down the sexiest chick you've ever seen when she's begging you to put your dick in her. I was weak."

I smirk at him. "She was fucking fine, though. Don't shoot, I'm just sayin'." I throw my hands up quickly.

He chuckles. "Brother, she's fucking outstanding."

When I arrive home, I drop my shit in the games room and grab a cold beer out of the bar fridge. Sitting on the sofa, I think over all the shit that's happened lately. I know I've fucked it for Vicky and me, and it couldn't fucking hurt more if someone stabbed me right in the fucking heart.

VICKY

Arriving home, I go straight up to our dorm and sink into my bed. I have cried enough tears for him—fuck Blake Rendon. I feel like I've been saying that a lot lately. I walk into the bathroom to take a couple of painkillers.

Not the bad kind, the good, safe kind.

Opening our pill cabinet that sits behind the mirror, I notice the tampons, which immediately reminds me of my period. I begin adding the days in my head figuring out when I'll be due.

"Oh my fucking God!" Putting my hand over my mouth, I drop all the pills on the ground. There's no way, I just finished my period the day I was driving to Coronado, and surely you can't get pregnant that quick? I'm on the mini pill too. I know that the mini pill is not as effective as the full contraception pill, but it's the only one that doesn't make me feel like I want to rip everyone's heads off.

Picking up my keys from the bench, I make my way to the store. I've always dreaded the day that I'd need to buy a fricking pregnancy test.

Please be a false alarm.

After the walk of shame of buying a pregnancy test off the young, snotty uptight bitch from behind the counter, I'm currently back home and sitting waiting for a single little line to appear in the little window. I look down at my phone, seeing three minutes have passed, so I pick up the stick that holds my fate and look down.

"FUCK! "Fuck, fuck, *fuckity fuck!"* I scream. After the anger dissipates, I begin to cry for the second time today. Putting my hands over my face, I slide down the walls until the cold tiles are under my ass.

You'll get piles that way, Vicky.

I don't care at the moment. I don't care about fucking piles or fucking anything. I need to talk to Alaina, but I know she has so much going on right now and I don't want to stress her out with my shit as well.

Picking myself up off the floor, I make my way to my room, flop down on my bed and cry myself to sleep.

The next morning I wake up with a seedy stomach. I sit up in bed, cradling my stomach and make it to the bathroom just in time.

"Gross!" I wipe my mouth and move to the bathroom sink to wash my mouth out with mouthwash. Looking in the mirror, I try to push out my tummy to make it look big.

Fuck! I am going to get fat.

My mom didn't put on any weight with my brothers and me, but my Aunt Wilder? Man, she went full whale so I could go either way. My thoughts make me begin to cry *again.*

Pull your fucking self together, Abrahams.

You don't cry. Remember?

Flushing the toilet and washing my hands, I go out to my room and pull on track pants and a vest before making my way to my first class. I usually care what I look like out in public, but seeing as people are going to start talking about me soon enough, they may as well start now. I walk into class and pull out a seat next to Hailey. I've known Hailey for a couple years, she's a good person, and that's all I really care about in a friend.

"Vicky?" she whispers next to me, looking worried. "Are you okay?" she asks. I look at her with my puffy red eyes and nod.

"Yeah, I'm good." I say in a raspy voice, it feels raw from all the crying.

She looks away, but I know she doesn't believe me. I turn my head to the back of the room where I know Jesse usually sits. When he sees me, you can tell he wants to say something, but he knows I'm upset so he just leaves it. Which is a good thing, considering I'm not really in the mood to talk right now.

After class, I quickly pack up my bags and scramble out that door so fast, before anyone can start asking me one hundred and one questions.

Making my way home, I slam the door to our apartment and lock it. Then make way to my room ready to once again cry my eyes out and feel sorry for myself. My phone vibrating in my pocket distracts me from my moping, and when I see it's Alaina, I know I'm going to have to put on a happy face for her. The girl has a sixth sense when it comes to reading people.

"Lainy!" I say, with complete fake joy. I'm always happy to hear from her, but right now, I just want to be alone.

"I need to get drunk and get beautiful, or at least attempt it. And I need to be felt up by some hot sexy stranger." I giggle at her words wondering what Zane has done now. His list is growing mighty long.

"Well, as far as greetings go, I think that one's my favorite. I'll come pick you up now?" I am going to attempt to enjoy my one last night of not looking pregnant. I almost want to cry all over again at the thought of having cankles.

"Thank you! I could kiss you right now."

"I might take you up on that. See you soon." Hanging up my phone, I dress into some more appropriate clothes, because if Alaina saw me in what I'm wearing right now, she'd know straight away that there's definitely something going on.

The drive to the clubhouse is not long, and before I know it I'm pulling into the gates. I look over to the doors and see Alaina storm out like someone just stole her toys. *Not like her at all.* She curls her finger to one of the pretty prospect boys, making his shoulders slump in defeat before getting onto his bike. Once we hit the highway, my curiosity gets the better of me.

"Are you good?" I ask, glancing at her in the passenger's seat.

"Yeah, I'll be fine. I'm just so confused. I miss my uncomplicated life."

I laugh. "But your *'uncomplicated life'* didn't include a drop-dead-sex-on-two-wheels biker?"

Don't I know about an 'uncomplicated life.'

"Drop-dead-sex-on-two-wheels, *married* biker," she replies.

I slam on my breaks and swerve to the side of the road. "Holy fuck, Vicky. What the hell is wrong with you? One little incident and Bumboy behind us will call it in!"

I *cannot* believe I didn't pick it up.

"That fucking piece of slimy shit! I don't care about those pretty green eyes, or those perfect dimples, or that hellish smirk. Homeboy is going down." Alaina laughs and it softens me a bit. She has a tendency to do that.

"You know I love you, right?" I tap her on the knee.

"I love you too, girl."

Getting back on the road, I look behind us and see Bumboy is still following close behind. I smirk because these boys have no idea how much work Alaina and I are when we are together.

No idea.

We walk back into our apartment and it reminds me of all the realities that are happening to me right now. But even more so of the severity of my situation.

I am going to be a solo mom.

I almost crack right then and there. If it weren't for Alaina walking out with a bottle of Jägermeister, I would have. She hands me a drink, and I pretend to sip on it until she walks out the room then it goes straight down the sink. I can't say that I'm not drinking tonight, she'll work it out and I can't lie to her. I definitely *cannot* lie to this girl.

She walks out after her shower, pouring *another* shot.

Oh, fuck! I'm going to have my work cut out for me tonight.

"Okay Vick, I want *come get it* mixed with *but will I give it?* Help me?" I have no idea what she's on about, but I smile a cheesy smile because I know the exact dress that she will pull off.

"I know just the piece." Following me to my room, I pull open my wardrobe and start throwing clothes out over my shoulder. It's not like it was one hundred percent in order before anyway. Life is too short to worry about how fucking tidy things are, as long as you're clean, it's good.

Shit could be worse. I mean, you could wake up one day and be a pregnant solo-mom-to-be, to a biker who doesn't even want you. Saying that in my head makes it sound just as bad as it is.

Oh boy, what the fuck have I gotten myself into this time? Daddy cannot buy me out of this dilemma.

I freeze in my thoughts. Fuck! I hadn't even thought of my damn parents. They're going to be so disappointed in me. My brothers Dominic and Jacob will probably want to drive here to bury Blake, too.

Yeah, right.

My brothers may be big men, but there's no way they'll have a chance in hell with someone as ruthless as Blake. You only have to look at Blake to see the death that sits behind his eyes. His eyes are as black as his soul. When he's with me, he is different.

Well, at least I thought he was.

"Ah ha! Here it is," I say to Alaina, as I'm pulling the little white dress out from its hibernation spot. "This will look perfect with your *fuck me* boots."

She fluffs it out in front of her and looks at me. "Yes, exactly what I need."

After I put on my trusty tight little black dress and stilettos and leaving my hair dead straight as it falls past my waist, I make my way into the kitchen. "Are we ready?"

She nods while picking up her clutch. "Definitely."

I drive us there because I know that can now be my excuse as to why I'm not drinking. We pick Hailey up on the way because she's adamant she wants to come with us, probably just to quiz me to see what's wrong with me. Walking into the bar, I roll my eyes at all the stares coming from the men. Usually, I'd be all over the attention, but since Blake blew up my life, I've not been interested.

The baby thing fucks it up, too.

I'm keeping an eye on Alaina, who's currently putting too many drinks away. Zane must have really worked a number on her. I give her eyes that say, *'slow the fuck down,'* feeling a lot like a hypocrite but not caring at all.

"Oh my fucking God. Who is that?" Hailey asks, looking over at Hunter, a.k.a Bumboy.

"Oh, him?" Alaina asks casually. "That's my babysitter. You like?" She wiggles her eyebrows, making me almost spit my water out everywhere. I hate it when she does that, her eyebrows move so perfectly that it's scary.

"Mmm, I like," Hailey responds as she makes her way over to him.

I shake my head in disapproval. Nothing good can come from liking a biker.

Well, apart from a baby.

Alaina's yanking my arm toward the dance floor interrupts my thoughts. Holy fuck the girl has some serious power behind her little frame. I follow her onto the floor as we start booty dancing to Trick Trick's *'Twerk Dat, Pop That.'* I drop it low, bringing it back up. I'm laughing as I swing my head around, grinding up onto Alaina and that's when I see Blake. I'm almost certain that my whole world stops as panic sets in. Pulling away from Alaina, I dodge the crowd trying to get as far away from Blake or any of them as quickly as possible.

I'm aware leaving Alaina in the crowd is a shitty thing to do, but I know that as long as Zane is around she's perfectly safe. I push open the exit doors and power walk to my car, beeping it open. Quickly, I slide in and make my way back to the apartment.

Once I'm safely in the comfort of my little home, I kick my shoes off and strip out of these ridiculous clothes, noticing that they are a little tight around my stomach area. I walk into my room, slide under my covers and as I drift off to sleep, wishing that things were different.

BLAKE

I pull my drink, watching Brittney work her magic on the pole when I get a text from Hunter.

> Hunter: *Yo! You and Zane might wanna get down here ASAP. The girls are looking a bit out of control, brother. Fucking trouble, both of them.*

I narrow my eyes at my phone, squeezing it in my hand. I sit there for a few seconds, clenching my jaw together in frustration. “Fuck.” I get up off my chair, knowing that I won’t sleep tonight if I don’t know that she’s safe. I walk up to Zane’s office and see him deep in thought, smoking a cigarette.

“You been smoking a lot since a certain blonde Kiwi came into your life,” I say as I cross my arms in front of me, leaning on the doorframe.

He looks up to me as he’s blowing out smoke. “Tell me about it. Everything good?” he asks.

I shake my head. “I got a text from Hunter. The girls are up to no good.”

He pushes his seat back, putting his smoke out. “Let’s go.”

Walking into the club, I spot both of them instantly. With Alaina’s white hair, she’s hard to miss. I point over to them, and both Zane and I sit back and just watch. I laugh and look over at him.

“They have no fucking idea.” I notice that Zane isn’t responding to me, so I look closer, and see that his mouth is set in a thin hard line.

“Brother, she’s just hurting. Let her vent. If anything happens, we’ll step in.” I feel Ade push up next to me.

“Where the fuck did you come from?” I ask.

He shrugs. "Hunter text me what was happening, too. You know, to check on Alaina."

Zane turns his head to Ade. "I fucking told you. Stay away from her, Ade. I fucking mean it."

Ade throws his hands up. "Brother, I'm not interested in her like that. She's hot as fuck, don't get me wrong, but I love her like a sister. That's all."

I laugh while ordering our drinks. Ade has an enormous soft spot for Alaina, and it's caused major havoc in the Zane and Alaina bubble. Drinking my drink, I feel someone sit down beside me. I look over to see a sexy as fuck woman, with jet-black hair pulled up into a high ponytail. Any other day I would be riding her all the way home.

"Hey," she says, looking at me through drunken eyes.

"Hey," I respond, with no interest in her at all.

"You usually come here?" she asks, pulling her drink to her lips and licking the salt off the rim. I look at her with a bored expression.

"Nope, first time." I turn around, resting my shoulders on the bar. She comes over and puts her hand on my chest.

"Wanna get out of here?"

Typical uptight bitches. They all want the bad boy biker experience, only to run for the hills when shit gets real.

"Nah, I'm good," I reply bluntly, as I push off the bar and make my way back to Zane and Ade.

I look back to Alaina and Vicky and see Vicky booty hopping all over the place, making my dick hard instantly. "Fuck," I mumble under my breath, as I readjust myself. She turns her head, laughing, but when her eyes find mine her smile drops instantly.

Pushing my way through the crowd, I'm eager to get to her. I drive through everyone, but I can't find her. Turning my head just in time I see Zane rip Alaina out of the hands of some douchebag in the middle of the dance floor.

"Oh shit." I launch myself back in that direction, ready to fuck some shit up. Ade and I stand there for a little while, letting Zane do what he needs to do, before pulling him off. He throws Alaina over his shoulder and walks out, with Ade and me following closely behind. On our way out, I text Vicky. I need to see her, it's as though she has my cock on a leash.

VICKY

When I wake, it's still dark outside. I get up to get a head start on my day because I need to visit the doctor and see exactly what's going on. Then I'll tell Alaina. Pulling my phone off the nightstand, I notice I have a text message. My heart almost leaps out of my chest when I see it's from Blake.

> Blake: *I know you hate me, but did you get home ok?*
> Blake: *Dammit, Vicky. Stop being so fucking stubborn and just answer me.*

I throw my phone onto the bed in frustration. How can a man make you hate him, but love him at the same time? Gasping, I throw my hands up to my mouth.

"I fucking love him, don't I?" Well, if this is love then the fairy tales lied and I'm about to sue *Disney* for giving me false hope in men.

Pouring my morning coffee, I stop mid pour, realizing that I can't even drink coffee. "Fuck my life," I mutter as I tip it out, making a hot cocoa instead. I need that Milo shit that Alaina used to go on about. Maybe a trip to New Zealand could be on my bucket list. Thinking about telling Blake that I'm pregnant makes me feel physically sick. He's going to hate me. Pulling my pants on and zipping up my hoodie, I call my doctor. Lucky for me, he can see me in half an hour.

Sitting in the doctor's surgery, everything feels surreal. There are pregnancy catalogs spread out everywhere, and when I see the little babies on the front of them, it freaks me out. I can't believe I'm going to be responsible for another life! I can't even look after myself.

"Victoria Abrahams?" A young, tall, perky nurse comes out from the reception area. I get up out of my seat and make my way to her. "Dr. Nesh will be with you shortly. Please take a seat," she tells me as she leads me into his office.

I sit in the seat that's opposite his. A few moments later, the doctor walks in. He's in his mid to late fifties and the best pre-natal doctor that's currently practicing in our area.

"Hello Victoria, what can I do for you?" he asks as he leans in to shake my hand. He then takes a seat in his big important chair. I take a deep breath before I begin.

"I'm pregnant. I think. I mean, I took a pregnancy test and it said...you know? That I'm pregnant."

Wow, Vicky, you sound very smart right now.

I watch his face and he's trying not to show shock. He knows my mother and father, and he knows that this can't be a good thing.

"Okay," he says. "Jump up on the bed so I can have a feel around your stomach." I get up onto the bed as he asks pulling up my top as he starts to press down on my stomach.

"I'm going to do a scan. Is that okay? You feel quite far along, so you can have an ultrasound. You won't need a TVS."

I pause. "Really? Okay, let's do it then." Thinking over how many periods I have missed but coming up short. My periods have always been irregular, it was not out of the norm for me to miss a month.

After seeing my little baby on the screen, and hearing its little heartbeat, I know I'll never be able to go through with a termination.

Pulling out into the traffic, I do a U-turn and make my way to the clubhouse. I need to vent. On arrival, I make my way out of my car quickly and walk into the bar area.

Shit, it's so nice in here.

I see Harvey first and ask him to point me in Alaina's direction, which he does. Once I find her room, I push open the door and sit down on her bed, waiting for her to come out.

"Holy shit, Vicky!" she yells, clutching her towel in front of her when she walks into the room.

"I need to tell you something, and it's not good...*at all.* And I don't know what to do," I say to her, fidgeting with my fingers.

"Okay, I'm listening?" I look up to her as a tear breaks out of my eye and rolls down my cheek.

"I'm pregnant, Lain. *Fucking pregnant!"* I almost scream, throwing my hands in the air.

"What! Are you sure? When did you find out?" She looks shocked, her face has gone white and her eyes are wide and that's exactly how I thought she'd react. I decide to leave out that I found out yesterday because I know that she'll want to know why I didn't tell her straight away.

"Just this morning. I've been feeling a little sick lately, and I think I knew deep down that something wasn't right. But I was in denial, you know?" Saying it out loud makes it feel much more real.

"You disappeared last night, right before Zane went all *'Me Tarzan, you Jane'* on me," she says.

I nod my head. "I know, I noticed them come in and wanted to get away. I'm sorry, Lain. I tried to get your attention, but you were on *Project Be-A-Whore* so I couldn't. I'm so sorry. I know I'm a terrible friend for just ditching." I feel sorry about it, anything could have happened. If it weren't for the fact that Zane was there, I wouldn't have left her.

"Seriously, it's fine. Don't worry about it. I can't believe this, though. And it's Blake's? Not Jesse's or anything?" It would only be natural for her to ask me this, but Jesse and I haven't seen each other since before spring break and we always used a condom.

"Yes, it's Blake's. I haven't touched Jesse in months, since before summer break. Fuck Alaina, we haven't spoken to each other in two weeks, ever since I found out he was using me."

She pales, before starting to apologize. "Oh fuck, I'm so sorry. I forgot all about that. There's just been too much going on—"

I cut her apology off. "Lain, you have so much drama going on, it's fine. You didn't do anything wrong."

She sits beside me on the bed. "What are you going to do? I'll support you whatever you decide to do. You know that, right?" I smile. This is exactly why I can never live without this girl.

"I know. I'd better get going, but how was the rest of your night?" I ask. Her face lights up like Christmas.

Say no more.

"It was...surprising."

Laughing as I make my out of her room, eager to get the fuck out of there before Blake comes back, I quickly poke my head back into her room. "Please don't say anything to Zane. I haven't told Blake, and I haven't figured out what I'm going to do yet. I might just head to the ranch for a bit and turn my phone off until I figure everything out. If you need me, call the ranch phone number." I decide right then and there that I want to go and spend some time at our family ranch. Well, it was our family ranch until the divorce. Now it's where my dad and his *girlfriend* live. He'll not get in my way, and I'll just hide in the guesthouse.

"Of course, Vick. I love you."

"I love you too."

Pulling off my coat and hanging it up behind our door, I grab my phone out of my pocket and instantly dial my dad's number.

"Jefferson speaking," a voice greets me.

That stern voice still hasn't changed.

"Dad? It's Vicky." After a few minutes of catching up, because my dad always has a lot to ask and say when I call him, I start packing up my things. Making sure that I have everything because I have no idea how long I'm going to be away for. Just as I put my phone into my bag, I notice a text message arrive.

Blake: *I am coming over.*

Moving in double time, I squash everything into my bag and run out to my car, not sparing any second glances at anything behind me.

That probably makes me look crazy.

It's not until I'm on the main highway that I relax. My family ranch is a long drive, over seven hours by car. So I make sure I stock up on heaps of supplies and water to keep me hydrated for the long trip.

Pulling up to our long gravel road I get out and check the mailbox out of habit, before carrying on up the huge, oversized driveway to the ranch. I begin pulling my bags out of the boot when I feel big arms wrap around my waist and lift me from my feet and I automatically know who it is.

"Dominic?" I squeal.

"Hey precious, how was your trip?" he grumbles, placing me back on my feet.

My brother is a giant of a man. He stands well over six foot three and must weigh in at around two hundred and twenty pounds of muscle. He owns one of the largest gyms in the Hollywood hills.

"Oh my gosh, when did you get here?" I ask, as he picks up my bags and I follow him into the house.

"Yesterday. Dad needed some help around the place because he fired the last boy he had working here. The new one starts in two days, so I'm here to help until then." Typical Dad behavior, he fires everyone. He obviously thinks he's *Donald* flipping *Trump.*

"I'll go put these in your room."

I shake my head. "In the guesthouse please, I need some space."

He looks at me with worry lines forming around his eyes. "Okay, is everything good?"

Nodding my head, I glance away from him for a second. "Yeah, of course."

Walking into the large living room area, I see my Dad sitting in the rocking chair with a whiskey in his hand, looking apprehensive.

"Hey Dad," I say, peeking up at him. He shoots up off his seat with shock in his eyes.

"Hey precious, I'm so glad you made it." I knew he would have been worried about my traveling, nothing much changes in the eyes of a loving father. He may have fallen out of love with my mom, but he never stopped loving us kids. It will take time on my behalf though, because he shouldn't have cheated on my mother. He could have just left.

"Of course, I did. All those driving lessons didn't go to waste, you know." He smiles a big grin down at me, and for the first time in a long time I see how much he's aged. That feeling pulls at my heartstrings.

"Very good. I hope your taste in music still stands?" I laugh at his question while taking a seat on one of the other sofas.

"Still very much alive, Dad."

Sitting back into his seat and taking another drink, he smiles around the rim of his glass. "How is Alaina?" My family love Alaina. They took her under their wing from day one, not that she needed it. Alaina had an unyielding support system with her Nana and Aunt.

"She's good, really good. She has a boyfriend now, though."

Dominic walks in at the mention of Alaina. "Alaina has a boyfriend? Do tell." He smiles while eating some peanuts.

"He is....interesting."

Dominic's face drops. "Good interesting or bad interesting?"

I have to be careful with how I word anything to do with Alaina around Dom. I always forget that he was Alaina's *first time*. I almost killed them both when it happened. I didn't talk to either of them for weeks until I got over it.

"Hmmm, hard to say. He does really like her, so that's all that matters." I stand from the sofa and stretch out my arms.

"I'm going to go and get settled in." Dominic looks at me with a smirk.

"Sis? Stay away from Knox when he starts, too." I slump my arms back down and huff.

"Ha ha, very funny. You make me sound like a man-eater. I can assure you, I *will* be staying away." His chest moves up and down from his laughter.

"Well, I wouldn't—" I snap my eyes at him with a sneer.

"Shut up Dom, don't be mean. I'm not like that anymore."

He laughs and raises his eyebrows. "Oh yeah? Then tell me, how was spring break with Kalie?" I look at him with my chin held high, I forgot how close those two are. They drive me crazy, the both of them.

"It was...something that you probably don't want to hear about." I turn and make my way toward the guesthouse before I say something completely sassy that *will* end up getting me into trouble.

I walk past the back garden that looks well kept. It makes me sad because this was my mom's favorite part of the entire house. I continue past the massive pool and into the guesthouse. Turning on the lights, I notice everything is still the same. Looking very much like a bachelor pad, because my brothers always stay in here when they're back home. I put my bags down and pull out my phone to turn it off. I see I have ten missed calls and two texts from Blake. Deciding not to open them, I turn my phone off and place it in the top drawer where it will reside the end of my stay.

The next day, I open my eyes and stretch out my arms. I'm feeling sicker than I did yesterday, so I dash off to the bathroom. Walking out back into my room, I throw on a summer dress and put my hair in a loose fishtail braid then make my way into the main house to find my brother. Opening the back door, I see Dom standing there talking to a young guy that has a smile to die for.

"Hey, want to go for lunch?" I ask my brother, who's looking between both me and the sexy man standing in the kitchen.

"Yeah, give me a minute precious." I smile and start to make my way outside. The staring from the hottie doesn't go un-noticed either. I get into my car and wait for Dominic patiently. He takes around five minutes before he comes out. Stopping in his tracks, he shoves his hands into his pocket and tilts his head to the side. He then hitches his thumb into the air in the *'get out'* motion.

Rolling my eyes, I jump out of my car and ask, "What?"

He walks toward the garage, opening the door and showing me Dad's old 1967 Camaro.

"Oh, I forgot all about her. Did you do her up?"

He smiles a wide grin. "Sure did."

I begin to get into the passenger seat when he stops. "What, now the precious daughter wants to play princess? Since when do you *not* want to drive, Vick? Get in the driver's seat." I laugh while walking back over to him, snatching the keys from his hand.

"Please, of course not. That'll never change." I slide into the driver's seat, firing her to life. Feeling the deep rumble of the V8 from under my seat is amazing. I clap my hands in excitement while looking at my brother, who's laughing in the passenger seat. I begin pulling out of the garage just as my dad starts walking out onto the porch. He looks over to us, smiling. I notice straight away as the realization hits him because his face turns serious all of a sudden.

"Dominic! You get her out of that seat right now. That's too much power for her."

I giggle, looking over to my brother. "Should I?"

He laughs, rubbing his chin while nodding his head. "Yeah, do it."

So I drop the clutch and start to rev the loud engine while waiting for my RPM's to come up, then I floor the gas and release the clutch as the front tires lock up and the back tires start spinning, creating smoke clouds instantly. Dominic and Jacob taught me how to do a burnout when I was ten, but my dad has no idea. I hear yelling coming from the house, but I can't see anyone because of all the smoke that clouds the surrounding area around the inside and outside of the car. Dominic and I are laughing our asses off, I love working Dad up. Deciding that I still need my dad alive, I stop and let the car idle on the spot. Once the clouds of smoke disperse, I see my dad standing there with his hands on his hips and a small smile on his lips.

"Well, I'll be damned. My baby girl knows how to drive." He can't even be mad. Between him and my brothers, there was no way I was ever going to come out playing with dolls and riding scooters.

I'm still laughing when I see the young guy standing up against our porch pillars. He's smiling at me with a toothpick in his mouth. I grin back at him.

"Who is that?" I ask, nudging my head over to the big, brown-haired, tanned beauty. Dominic looks to me and laughs. "That's what you're staying away from. Dad only just hired him this morning. Once you leave, he'll move into the guest house." I raise my eyebrows in surprise. Dad usually doesn't hire the young ones, probably to keep them away from his whore of a girlfriend. I put the car into first and begin to drive out of the driveway. *Responsibly.*

We're sitting at the café ordering food, and I notice all the girls looking at Dominic. I roll my eyes. I should be used to it by now, both of my brothers are exquisite looking men, but it still annoys the shit out of me.

"I need to tell you something," I say to him as he's glancing through the menu.

"Yeah? All right. Shoot."

I raise my hand up. "First of all, you're not to tell Dad or Mom. And definitely not Jake." Dominic is my eldest brother, so he's all responsible and easy to talk to. Jacob, though? He's bossy, controlling and a pain in my ass. Both my brothers and my dad have always been fiercely protective of me, but Jacob takes it to some next level shit, and that's why he cannot know what I'm about to tell Dominic.

"That bad, huh?" he asks, taking a drink of his water. I can see his eyes harden as he mentally prepares himself for my confession.

"I'm pregnant." His face scrunches up, while his jaw ticks. I know he's pissed, but he's my big bear of a brother who can't be mad at me for long.

"Vicky, fuck's sake. Who the fuck is the dad?" I put some food into my mouth to delay the next thing that's going to set him off.

"Um, I don't think that's relevant right now—"

"Vicky. Who. The. Fuck. Is. The. Dad," he repeats emphasizing each word, clenching his jaw tighter.

I sigh in defeat. "Blake Rendon. We spent the summer together, and he got me pregnant. He was different to my other hook ups, though. I felt something for him." His face softens a bit.

"So you are together then?"

I clear my throat. "Not exactly. He's a member of a motorcycle club and—"

He cuts me off again. "You're fucking with me? Tell me you're fucking with me, Vicky!"

I shake my head and butt back in before his mind goes wild with unnecessary thoughts. "No Dom, he's not like that. He's not grungy and gross. *And* before you get mad at me, Alaina is seeing the president, just saying." Okay, that wasn't my finest hour, throwing my best friend under the Dominic bus, but I need to get the heat taken off me for a second. I watch him as a few emotions pass over his face, settling back into a soft smile.

"All right, it's going to be okay. I think…" he pauses for a second then looks up to me. "I'm going to be an uncle?" He smiles proudly.

"Yes. You big bear…you're going to be an uncle." After that, our lunch goes smoothly. We talk and chat like we always do. I love having big brothers. Thinking of that, reminds me that I'm going to have to tell Jacob.

"How is Kalie?" I ask around a mouthful of food. If my appetite was big before, it's ginormous now.

"She's good. She's been creating waves in the Hills with her moves. The girl is going to be huge." I nod my head in agreement. Kalie's a professional dancer. Not the stripper kind, the kind that has her dancing for all sorts of famous people in their music videos.

"She is. We had heaps of fun over the holiday," I say, smiling at the memories. Dom looks up to me.

"What happened? Kalie didn't say much, she just said that it was unforgettable and that you were mischievous as usual."

I laugh. "Mischievous is probably a slight understatement."

He scrunches up his face and shakes his head. "Scratch that, I don't want to know."

I always used to think that Dom and Kalie would make a good couple. Some would think they had something going on, but it's not true. He cares about her like a sister. I wonder how he'd feel if he found out about a biker deflowering her? I think he'd hate all bikers for life.

Better keep that one to myself.

Walking through the front door, the smell of home baking arouses my senses. I make my way into the kitchen and see Beverly's in there baking up a storm. Beverly Scott is my dad's...whore. She basically broke up my parents' marriage. I know that it takes two and all that, but she'll always be the evil bitch that used to come around to my house pretending to be my friend just so she could flaunt her little ass around my dad. Yep, that's right, she's the same age as me.

"Wow Bev, would never have taken you for the baking type. Didn't know they taught baking at the cock sucking school for whores," I say innocently at her with a smile.

"Nice to see you too, Vicky. Good to see you still haven't changed." I walk past her and steal a muffin.

"Ditto, Bev. It's nice to see you haven't changed either. You're still a walking skank with daddy issues."

I walk out smoothly before I blow up in her face and scratch out her box. I bump into a rock hard chest on my walk back to the guesthouse. Looking up, I see it's the worker hottie.

"Hi, sorry. I should've been watching where I was going," I apologize, looking up at him. He laughs, rubbing his hand over his five o'clock shadow, my eyes following his movements.

If I weren't pregnant, I would be tearing that ass up.

"No problem. Victoria, is it?" he asks with a tiny smile on his beautiful, square jaw.

"Yes...um yup. Just Vicky though. You can just call me, Vicky."

Pull yourself together woman, shame on you.

"I'd better go." I quickly scramble into the guesthouse, panting like a child. Shit, he's really, *really* hot. Not in the same way as Blake, because Blake has his own level on the hotness scale. But more in an obvious, classic, attractive way. He looks like a gentleman.

I should have had his babies.

Over the next couple of days, I realize that I've not glanced at my phone once. The need to check it has become stronger and stronger every day. But I know if I check it, I'll end up replying to Blake. I notice hot worker man working on one of the fences, so I make my way to him.

"Hi, I never did get your name?" I ask, smiling sweetly at him.

He chuckles while stopping what he was doing. "Knox, Knox Bowden." I can't help but notice his southern drawl. I shake his hand, as he holds it out for me to take.

"Nice to meet you, Knox. Are you from around here?" I ask while jumping up onto the fence in front of him.

"I'm from Bama actually. Just down here for a change of scenery." I look down at him, he's wearing a white wife beater, ripped worn jeans and cowboy boots.

"I know that feeling." We chat for a couple hours. He's so easy to talk to, and a really nice guy.

"How long are you planning on staying here for?" I ask, genuinely interested.

"Not sure. I guess if I have a reason to stay, I might make my trip last longer," he replies with a smile on his face and a twinkle in his eye. I smile down at him as he makes his way closer to me, so he's eventually standing in between my legs. He reaches up and tucks a strand of hair behind my ear. "You're so beautiful, Vicky." I push my head back into his touch and closed my eyes, opening them when I feel soft lips touch mine. I know I should push him away because I'm carrying another man's baby, but it's too good to stop. Opening my mouth, I let him in while he licks around the rim of my lips. His kiss is soft and gentle, and before I let it get any further I stop and hold my hand up against his chest.

"I can't do this. As much as I *want* to, I can't," I tell him, looking down to the ground.

"I shouldn't have done that, I just couldn't help it," he replies.

Feeling like I should at least tell him why I stopped, I bite my bottom lip and look at him again. "I'm pregnant, that's why. It's all really messy and I'm not with the father, but I just can't have any complications in my life right now." Nice, now he'll go running for the hills, and my dad will be down a worker.

Good job, Vicky.

He tilts his head, making the afternoon sun hit his skin perfectly, and he smiles at me. "So you don't have a boyfriend?"

Laughing before looking back to him. "Did you not just hear what I said? I'm pregnant."

He laughs and shakes his head. "I don't care. Not only are you beautiful, but the time we've spent talking together has made me see you differently. Nothing can change that."

I jump off the fence, noting that I cannot feel my ass. "What time do you finish?" I ask him.

He looks down at me, bringing his hand under my chin and running his thumb over my bottom lip slowly. "Five. I promised your father that I'd cook dinner tonight. Care to help?" he asks with a smile.

I nod my head and bite my lip. "Yes, that sounds like fun. I love to cook." He brings my hand up and kisses it gently before I head back inside the house. He's amazing. There's no doubt about that. He gives me butterflies and good feelings.

Maybe I should give it a try with him, without putting a label on it.

Walking into the kitchen, smiling at the memory of his soft lips pushed against mine, I see Dominic sitting at the table. His arms are crossed over his chest and his eyebrows are raised.

This is not good.

"What part of *'stay away from him'* did you not understand? And for fuck's sake Vicky, *you're pregnant!*" he almost yells from where he's sitting. And Dom never yells.

"First of all, you can't tell me who to stay away from. We were just talking...and stuff. Second, he knows I'm pregnant, Dom! I'm not some shady bitch, so keep your judgments to yourself," I reply, shutting the fridge door.

"He knows you're pregnant and he doesn't care?" he asks in disbelief.

I laugh at him. "Dom, it's not like we're actually an item or anything. Nothing's happened and nothing is going to happen. Let me be." I walk out of the kitchen and head back to my room, needing some distance from an annoying brother. I feel like

I am fifteen again, and crushing on Brad Levitt, my hot neighbor.

After hibernating in my room, listening to music, I get up and make my way into the main house to help Knox with dinner. I'm walking out when I see him walking across to me.

"Hey, I was just about to come in and help you," I say to him.

"Thought I'd come get you," he says smiling down at me. He lifts my chin and looks deep into my eyes. "I wanna kiss you so bad, but I won't, not until I know you want me to." I smile and nod my head.

"Thank you," I reply before we head into the main house.

We walk into the kitchen to get started on dinner. Deciding on spaghetti bolognese, because it's Dom's favorite. I like to apologize to people through cooking.

"So, is it just you and Dominic?" Knox asks while chopping up tomatoes.

"I have another brother too, Jacob. But he lives back in Hollywood Hills, running his empire in the music department. He's a music producer and a great one at that." I realize I've been rambling on, so I turn my attention back to him.

"What about you? Do you have any siblings? They're just *great,* I tell ya," I say the last part with sarcasm. He laughs while adding the red wine into the pot. I notice that he's done all the cooking.

"I have two sisters. They're a pain in the ass." I laugh while pouring a glass of water.

"I'm pretty sure that all brothers just say that."

He nods while laughing, "Probably."

Draining the spaghetti, he comes in behind me. "What's your favorite color?" he whispers into my ear. I smile a bright smile.

"That's easy…blue. What's yours?" I ask, turning around to face him.

"It was red, but now I think I like the color brown just that much more," he responds, looking into my eyes. I smile at him and pick out the plates so we can set the table.

CHAPTER 15

After a really awkward dinner, because Dom was throwing glares at Knox, we begin walking back to the guesthouse.

"Thanks for dinner. I know you did all the cooking. How'd you learn to cook like that?" I ask, looking up at him as the moonlight hits the pool and bounces up onto his face making me notice all the perfect curves and lines. He sits down beside the pool, bringing his hand up to mine and tugging me gently, so I sit beside him.

"My mom. She wanted to make sure that I could cook because, in her words, a kitchen isn't just for women." He laughs, looking up at the sky. It's at that moment that I realize maybe she's not here anymore. He continues, "She passed away a couple of years ago. Car accident on the way back from a rodeo. Life hasn't really been the same since, so

I've just been drifting around the place." I look up to him and bring my palm to his face, pushing him to face me.

"I'm sorry, I couldn't imagine not having both parents." He smiles, bringing his hand up to my face and running his thumb across my cheek.

"You need to stop looking at me like that, or I will kiss you again." I'm looking deep into his eyes and I'm almost certain that I at least want to try it.

"Kiss me then. I want you to kiss me," I whisper.

With that, he pulls my face down to his and kisses me. I kiss him back, running my tongue over his until his hand comes up and he wraps his fingers around the back of my neck. He stops and begins pulling away from me.

"Yeah, we should probably stop." I blush instantly and look down to the water.

"No. Hey!" He reaches for my face. "Not because I want to, but because I don't wish to push anything."

I smile at him. "I didn't know men like you still exist."

He laughs, getting back onto his feet and helping me up. "Maybe just not where you were looking." He's right, I've never found the real sweet guys attractive. Maybe I should have, and then maybe I wouldn't be knocked up right now.

"I'll see you tomorrow?" I ask him, hoping he'll say that he's working.

"I'll see you tomorrow," he replies, kissing me on the forehead and leaving.

I make my way to bed, and after thinking over a lot of things I realize one thing's for sure I miss and love Blake like crazy. There is absolutely no way that I can use Knox as a rebound for my hurt.

The next morning I wake up feeling like shit. I know I need to end whatever's going on between Knox and me before one of us gets hurt. I'm walking into the house when I hear the phone ringing, catching it just in time.

"Hello, Abraham's residence," I say in a bright tone because that's how you're supposed to answer the phone in this dysfunctional household.

"Vicky?" I hear Blake's voice on the other end of the phone, and just as I'm about to put the receiver down he continues, "Vicky, stop! Do not fucking hang up on me!" I keep the phone to my ear but don't say anything.

"Alaina got kidnapped. We're in New Zealand right now, but I thought I'd let you know that she's okay."

I suck in a breath. "What? Oh my God, Blake! *Oh, fuck!*" I'm starting to panic, clutching the phone in my hand when Knox walks in.

"You all right, darling?" he asks, coming up next to me and kissing me on the forehead.

I hear Blake growl down the phone. "Vicky that better be one of your fucking brothers." His accusations make my panicking stop as I walk out of the room.

"Well, no it's not. His name is Knox, and he's the hired help here for a few weeks." I don't care what he says. After all, what can he do from all the way from New Zealand? And he's made it *very* clear that we can see other people.

The line goes deathly quiet for a second. "Are you fucking him?"

I look at the phone in my hand with a disgusted look. "Pardon? No, as a matter of fact I'm not." I smile at myself briefly before continuing, "But when I do *fuck him*, it will be none of your business. Because, remember Blake? You were the one that set down the *open relationship* rules. But know this, I have kissed him a couple times. Good fucking thing I'm not in a relationship, huh?" Shit, I didn't really mean to tell him about the kisses. The voice that comes down the phone chills me to the bone.

"I will fucking kill him, Vicky. So I hope that kiss was worth it." Then the line goes dead. I hang up the phone, walk back into the kitchen and look over to Knox.

"Yeah, I'll be okay. Just some drama back home is all." He nods his head before going back outside to finish up what he was doing. I run out to follow him. "Can I speak to you quickly?"

He turns around, the sun beaming directly behind him. "What's on your mind?" he asks. I start to fidget with my fingers. I've never cared about how I might hurt people's feelings before because those people were not Knox Bowden.

"I can't do this to you, it's not fair. I'm in love with the father of my baby, and it wouldn't be fair to you if I strung you along. You deserve so much better." I slump down onto the steps of the porch and he walks over, sitting down beside me.

"I can wait for you, Vicky. I will wait for you."

I shake my head. "Please don't, please don't wait for me. Blake is my happily ever after, even if I'm not his." A tear drops from my eye and I wipe it away quickly as he pulls me in under his arm, kissing my head.

"You're so special, Vicky. I'm sure he knows that. You'd have to be a fucking imbecile not to." I laugh at his comment.

"Thank you, Knox, for everything. For showing me that there are still decent men out there in this world." He kisses my head again before standing and going back to work. When I walk back into the kitchen my dad walks in too. He pulls open the fridge and grabs a bottled water then looks over to me.

"Vick, try to be nice to Beverly. I know you don't like her, but she rides my ass if you don't play nice." I scrunch up my face at my dad's choice of words.

"Ew Dad, that's gross. I need to talk to you, preferably with Mom, Dominic, and Jake in the room, too?" After taking a swig of his water, he nods his head.

"Okay, we can set them up on the speaker in my office. Everything okay?" Holy fuck, this man has no idea how *not okay* I am right now.

I smile. "Yes, perfect. I'll meet you in there in fifteen." Forgetting that it's probably some ungodly time in Paris, where my mom currently lives.

Fifteen minutes later, I walk into my Dad's office and sit on the seat next to Dominic. I can't stop jiggling my legs up and down, I'm that nervous. I look over to Dom and see that he's sitting there scratching his hand over his mouth, with a serious look on his face. I know he'll be worried about how this is going to go down. And just as I begin to second-guess my support system, he wraps his arm around my back pulling me under his arm.

Thank God for brothers.

My dad looks between Dominic and me, before settling on Dom. "You already know?" he asks, and Dominic nods his head. My dad picks up his phone and dials my mom and my brother Jake, both picking up at the same time.

"Sup Pops. What can I do for you?" You can hear girls in the background. I roll my eyes because that never changes, the man uses his good looks as a weapon.

Dad sighs. "Jacob? Dominic and Vicky are here too and your mother is also on the line. So get yourself somewhere that's far away from your flavor of the week." I hear Jake open and close a door before my mom speaks.

"Jefferson? What's going on? Put my daughter on the phone."

"I'm right here, Mom, everything's fine."

She breathes out loudly. "Oh good. How are you, darling? Why are you at the ranch? How is everything back there?" I laugh because my mother has an opinion on almost everything.

“I’m okay, Mom. You’ll know why I’m here in a second. The ranch is good, Dad hired a really, *really* hot worker the other day. Oh, Mom, he’s just—”

“*Vicky!* Cut the shit! What’s going on?”

That was Jake.

“Okay, the reason why I called this family meeting was to tell you all something. Before you all start freaking out, I’ve thought everything through, and please don’t kill me.” I take a deep breath and close my eyes. “I’m pregnant.” I blow out the breath that I’ve been holding in while I take in a lot of different things that are happening around me. The first thing is the swearing coming from Jacob’s end. *No surprise there.* The second thing is the disappointed look on my father’s face. *Well, he can talk.* The third thing is the complete silence coming from my mom’s end.

“Put my daughter on the phone. Just me and her,” she finally says. My dad, who still hasn’t said a word, picks up the phone and hands it to me.

“Hey, Mom.”

“Hey, baby. How are you feeling?”

This is new.

My mom and I have always been close, but I thought that she of all people would have lost her shit at me over this.

“I’m feeling okay, I have a bit of morning sickness, but it’ll pass.”

She giggles down the phone. "Much like me. I suffered horribly when I was pregnant with you. The boys, not so much. Who's the father?"

I clear my throat, taking a glance at my dad. "Um…his name is Blake. He owns a few different businesses, he doesn't know I'm pregnant yet, and he's a member of a motorcycle club." I squeeze my eyes closed expecting her to start screaming, but she doesn't.

"Okay, and are you two an item?"

She's so chilled about this. It's weird.

"No, we had a summer…thing. It sort of carried on once I got back to Westbeach, but we have a lot of issues and it'll never work out."

She exhales loudly. "All right, I'm obviously not overly happy with this news. I'm far too young to be a grandma, but I will come around just give me time."

A tear escapes my eye. "Okay Mom, thank you."

"Pass me to your father now, honey." I give the phone back to my dad, and glance down to the other phone that has Jacob on it.

"I'm not answering his question. Dom? Please?" He rolls his eyes before snatching up the phone. "Cut it, Jake, leave her alone." Their arguing dies out as I look up at my dad, who's standing there with his hands in his pockets.

"Dad? Say something." He sits down in front of me in his big business, flashy chair.

"I am in *no way* happy about this. But like your Mother, I *will* support you. You're just going to have to give me some time, too." I nod my head up and down. I didn't realize how much my father's opinion mattered to me until I saw the look in his eyes. "I think it's time for your mommy to tell your daddy about you. What you think little one?" I laugh at my brother's soft side coming out toward his little niece or nephew. At least if things turn to shit with Blake, I still have my family.

After saying goodbye to my family, and a heartfelt goodbye to Knox, I begin to make my way back home. I decide to turn on my phone for the first time since I got here, getting assaulted by text messages from Blake.

> Blake: *I'll be there soon, don't go anywhere.*
> Blake: *Vicky? Fuck sake answer your phone.*
> Blake: *Please answer your phone, baby. I need to talk to you, Vicky. Fuck sake.*
> Blake: *Fuck it then. Don't say I didn't try.*

"Shit." I sigh, pulling the gas nozzle out of my car and putting the lid back on. My phone starts ringing again in my pocket. I glance down expecting to see Blake, but it's not. Instead, it's my annoying brother.

"What do you want, Jake?" I ask, getting back into my car to have this conversation, because no doubt, it will include yelling.

"I don't understand it, and at the moment I don't like it, but I will grow to love it. Fuck, Vicky, why couldn't you just put your nose into your books?"

I roll my eyes. "I did, but stuff happens on spring break."

He breathes out loudly. "I'm going to come and see you when you have the baby."

"Okay, I'd like that. I love you."

He chuckles down the phone. "Yeah, I love you too, precious."

Hanging up the phone, I feel much better. If only things with Blake weren't so complicated.

After a long, seven-hour drive, I'm home and unpacking all my stuff. I get in the shower, wash my body, get out and dry off before falling straight into bed.

The morning sun attacks my eyes because I forgot to shut my curtains. Moaning, I get up and dressed in some casual clothes, noticing how big my bump is.

It's really a bump now. Shit!

I begin to make my way around campus, letting my teachers know that I'll be studying online for the rest of the year. The majority of them were polite about my obvious bump, except for my science teacher. I don't take it to heart, though, I can't fucking stand her. Once I arrive back home, I send a text message to Blake. I don't know where he is right now, but I hope he gets it.

> Me: *We need to talk. Come over when you are back.*

I throw my phone back down and cuddle up on the sofa, watching cartoons.

BLAKE

Walking into my house, I drop all my shit at the front door and go to my room. I got a text from my fucked up ex, saying that she wants to talk to me. Why this bitch won't just let me go, I do not know. After having a shower, I throw some clothes on and head back out the door to go sort this shit out with Corrin.

Pulling up to her apartment, I shut off my bike and walk to the door. After two knocks, she opens it and lets me in. I make it clear that I have no time for her shit straight away.

"What's this about, Corrin? I just got back in the country and you're the last person I want to see." She laughs while making her way into the kitchen.

"That's not very polite, Blake. Especially to someone that could end you and your little girlfriend with one tiny phone call to the Feds. I mean the ones that *aren't* working under your little whore of a police officer." She chuckles while pouring a drink.

I narrow my eyes at her. "What makes you think I won't just kill you, here and now?" I ask, walking over to her and snatching her drink from of her hands.

She tilts her head up to me with a smirk. "Because Blake, because you would never get away with it."

I laugh at her confidence. "Don't be too sure of that, pumpkin. You mention Vicky's name again and I'll put a bullet so far up your tight little ass, your brains will be painted on these fucking walls in a way that even Leonardo Da Vinci would be jealous of," I answer calmly. I see her gulp and her face drops for a few seconds, before returning to the bullshit look she's pulling now.

She looks back to me. “You know Blake, you’re not the only one that knows people.”

I grab onto her throat and push her up against the wall. “I don’t give a fuck who you know, Corrin. You so much as breathe my girl’s name again, and I’ll be back here with a shovel and a nine. Are we understood?” She doesn’t answer me, as she turns purple and I squeeze her neck harder. “I said…are we *fucking* understood?” She nods her head up and down, tapping on my hand to release her. I squeeze an inch harder before releasing her back to the floor. She coughs while holding onto her neck and I begin walking out the door before I hear her voice.

“You *will* pay for this Blake. You just wait.” I wish I could call her bluff, but I know she’s crazy. I also know that from this point onwards until I sort out who Corrin is using to bring my club and me down, Vicky has to stay away from it. We cannot be together under any circumstances, no matter how much I’m in love with her. And I *fucking love her* and *need her,* as if I need air to breathe. However, as the saying goes— the bad guys never get a happy ending.

After arriving home, I think over what’s happened between Vicky and me. I can’t fucking believe she kissed some other fucker, but I understand it. Popping open a beer, I see I have a text sent to my phone from an unknown number.

> Unknown: *There is always some madness in love. But there is also always some reason in madness.*

I throw my phone back on the bed, wondering why the hell I'm getting cryptic fucking texts at this hour. I look outside and notice a car parked outside my window. Picking my phone back up, I dial Corrin.

"Is this you? Do you think I'm fucking joking when I say that I will end you?"

She goes quiet for a second. "I don't care, Blake. If I can't have you, no one can."

I laugh. "What the fuck, Corrin? You're acting crazy. We ended a lifetime ago, and you knew that there was never going to be any more of us."

I hear her sob down the phone. "You loved me once, Blake. I was your everything at one point. Why can't we try again? It's because of *her,* isn't it? She's why you don't want me!"

I exhale loudly. "No Corrin, I didn't love you. I may have thought that I loved you, but now that I know what real love feels like, I know that what we had wasn't love. I love Vicky so much that it consumes me. So stay the fuck out of my way, or I'll bury you." I hang up the phone. A part of me feels bad for her. Corrin had a rough upbringing. She was in the system until she was eighteen. However, you cannot keep making excuses for people—she's a shallow, ruthless bitch, and that's all there is to it.

VICKY

The next morning I wake up in the same position I was in when I fell asleep, with my back aching in pain from being on the sofa. I rise up and try to get myself sorted. Just as I'm about to start calling around for apartments, the door swings open and Alaina walks in with bruises and a black eye.

"Lain! Oh my God!" I run over to her, taking her into a hug.

She smiles and rubs my bump. "Vicky! This is your decision?" I place my hand over hers. "It is, Lain. I want this baby, our baby. Only the thing is, I don't know how I'm going to break it to him."

She laughs while taking off her jacket. "Well, you'd better do it soon, because we're all back and he's on a mission to track you down."

Fuck! Shit!

I drop my eyes to the floor as the realization sinks in. "I know," I sigh. Then anger takes over my body when I remember what exactly has happened. "I can't fucking believe it, Alaina. You could have died! Tell me everything, right now." After that phone call from Blake, all I've been thinking about is her. She's going to put me in an early grave with the worry she causing me. It's probably a good thing that I never had any younger siblings.

"First, I need wine and pizza," she replies. I narrow my eyes at her, following her around the room.

"Pizza? You hate pizza."

"When you've had to go through not being fed, you'd love all kinds of food, too."

I pull two glasses out of the cupboard, one wine glass and the other, a regular one—the boring regular glass being for me. Thirty minutes later pizza boy shows up with the goods, and we settle into the sofa eating and laughing, just like old times.

"So, talk!" She goes into the gory details of her twisted life, from her life as a child, right up until she was kidnapped. I knew parts of her story but not all of it.

"Oh my God, is Jesse going to be okay? I can't believe it. It's like I have a sign on my head that flashes *'Use me to get to Alaina Vance'*." My self-esteem drops again.

"Don't be silly, he was working for my dad all along."

"I can't believe your father is some huge leader of the killer world, you're pretty badass! And your mom is alive? That's so beautiful, Lain. I'm so happy for you." I see her face light up, which warms my insides. I bite into my pizza.

"I'm really happy right now. Do you want ice cream?" she asks. I stop eating the pizza, even though the next bite is almost to my mouth.

"Ice cream?" I ask, with an eyebrow raised.

"Yeah, want some? I've still got some caramel in here somewhere." She starts shuffling through the freezer as if she hasn't been fed in months. I go silent. *I wonder if it's possible.* "Don't look at me like that. It's making me feel fat." I laugh at her ridiculous comment.

"When was your last period?" I ask her.

She pauses, spinning around to me. "What? I don't know. The night before I met Zane was when I finished. So over a month ago?" she whispers out the last bit in shock. "Fuck!" And with that single word I know, I just know, that she's pregnant. "No way! Keep your pregnancy bugs to yourself, I'm nowhere near ready for that shit."

I laugh while standing and take my plate to the sink. "Because of study? You finish up in two months, Alaina. You have a man that's head over heels in love with you. You could be worse off. For instance, having to drop school and hide the pregnancy from the father, because you know he never actually wanted you," I say that probably with a little too much emotion. The whole thing is fucked up and I'm feeling really insecure right now.

"Vicky, you need to speak to Blake. The way I see it, he does want you. Just talk to him, please. And get a jacket."

"Why?" I ask, putting another piece of this cheesy goodness in my mouth.

"I'm going to need a pregnancy test."

On our way to the drug store, I pull my phone out and see a text message from Blake.

Blake: *I'll come up later.*

That's the shortest text he's ever sent me. I send a quick reply.

Me: *Okay, see you then.*

We pull up to the drug store, and Alaina puts the car into park.

"Can you go in?" she asks with pleading eyes.

I laugh at her and shake my head. "No, they'll take one look at me and think, *well, isn't it obvious*. Go in, Lain. It's part of the whole pregnancy sucks thing." She huffs and walks off into the store.

Five minutes later, she comes back out carrying a pregnancy test and a bag of potato chips. I laugh as she gets back into the car.

"Don't laugh at me, Abrahams."

I hold in my breath to calm my giggles as she pulls out, and we make our way back home.

All I hear is crying coming from the bathroom, so I start knocking on the door.

"Lain? You okay?" I ask. She swings the door open, her eyes bloodshot red as she hiccups all over the place.

"No, it's positive. I'm pregnant."

I pull her into me and wrap my arms around her and start trying to reassure her. "It's going to be okay, Alaina. You have Zane, who loves you by the way, and everything's going to be all right."

She looks up to me, wiping the tears away from her eyes. "Promise?"

I squeeze her tight. "I promise. If not, we can be hot single moms in Bora Bora, having sex with random French men." She starts to laugh. I kiss her on the head and make my way into the kitchen to make us some green tea. It tastes like shit, but it's all we can drink.

We're sitting on the sofa watching television and I cannot stop thinking about Blake. I haven't seen him for almost a month, and I'm about to see him any minute now. A single knock comes from the door and I suck in a breath while making my way to it. Swinging it open, I see Zane standing there.

"Oh, Zane. Sorry. I thought you were Blake." I watch him as his eyes drop to my baby bump.

"Blake's?" he asks. I scrunch up my face and nod. He chuckles. "Good luck with that," he says while he walks off into Alaina's room.

Fuck, I really did NOT think this through.

Two hours have passed and Blake still hasn't showed up. By now, I'm itching at my fingertips, trying to busy myself with useless things around the house. It's just after ten when I hear another knock on the door, this time I open it to an incredibly sexy Blake. He smiles at me, running his fingers through his hair, making it messy. His eyes drop to my stomach, and he stills.

Here goes nothing.

He looks up at me with ice in his glare. "Mine?" he asks. I place my hand protectively over my stomach and nod.

"Sure is."

He brushes past me going straight into my room. After calling heads or tails on whether I should run or stay, I make my way into my room ready for the conversation of the year. I walk in and see him sitting on my bed. His elbows are resting on his knees, which are spread out in front of him with his head hanging low. I quietly close the door, sliding down it and sitting on the floor.

“What are you doing Vicky? Get on the fucking bed.”

I shake my head. “I’ll stay here, thanks though.”

A few seconds later, he rubs his hands up and down his face. “Were you even going to tell me?” I draw my knees up to myself, wrapping my arms protectively around them.

“Of course, I was going to tell you.” He stands up and sits opposite me on the floor, leaning against the foot of my bed.

“Can we do the parent thing without being together?” he asks, looking me right in the eyes. He must see me flinch because he drops his hands to his side and exhales quickly. “Fuck Vicky, you deserve so much more than me. I will fucking love my kid, and I’ll be there through everything with you, I promise you that. As a partner? I can’t tell you that I can one hundred percent be the man you need right now. I have so much fucking shit going on and you deserve better.”

I swallow down what feels like a ball of concrete. "Can I ask you something?"

He looks up to me with pain in his eyes. "Sure babe, what is it?"

I tilt my head sideways and squeeze my legs harder. "Did you ever feel anything for me?"

He reaches out with one hand, grabbing my hand and pulling me into him. "I fucking felt everything, babe."

He stands me up, deciding it's time for me to get into bed. Falling into be I snuggle into his side and fall asleep.

Waking up, I look at my clock, the face showing it's very early. I get up and make my way out to the living room, but stop in my tracks when I hear Zane and Blake talking.

"I want Vicky to move in with me until the baby arrives," Blake says.

I hear Zane shuffle. "You sure that's a good idea? I mean, you two haven't necessarily had the smoothest relationship."

"Yeah, I'm sure. My feelings for her are complicated, yes. But I want to be there for her through it all, and I want my kid."

"All right then brother, it's sorted. I'll ask Alaina to move in with me tomorrow." I slowly make my way back to bed and slump down into it. He's going to ask me to move in with him, and there's no way I can make this transition hard for Alaina. I know that if she senses trouble, she'll stay with me. I can't have that. She's about to have her own family now. I squeeze my eyes shut, forcing myself to go back to sleep.

I'm scrubbing up in the shower that morning, thinking over our conversation last night.

So what if I'm going to be a single mom. I'm going to rock this shit.

After overhearing Blake and Zane talking about me moving in with Blake, I decide to take advantage of the fact that I'm lucky that Blake isn't a deadbeat and agree with them. I'm still not sure how this is all going to work.

"Are you ready?" Blake asks as he carries all our bags down to his pickup truck.

"Yup. Yes, I'm ready," I say, walking over to him. He comes over to pick me up and help me into the truck.

"Yeah, no homeboy, I'll walk. I don't want to hurt you."

He stops and looks down at me. "Vicky, don't be stubborn and let me help you into the truck."

I pull myself up into my seat. "See, no help. Save the caveman bullshit for the Barbie sluts that need it. I'm a strong, independent woma—" He cuts me off by slamming the door. "Well, that was rude," I mumble to myself as he gets into the truck. He looks over to me with a serious look on his face and eyebrows raised, daring me to say something back to him. I drop my mouth and shrug,

"I'm not even mad."

He drags his eyes back to the front of him, pulling out onto the main highway.

"This should be interesting."

It has been one whole month since I moved in with Blake, and I have tripled in size. Living with Blake has been difficult at times, but he's never home anyway. The only time I see him is on nights when he gets home from *club business.* My little girl and I have our own room here, and I love it. Blake treats me well, as a loving, caring father should, but that's where it ends. I'm sitting at the kitchen table eating breakfast and looking for apartments when Blake bursts through the door. Alaina has been making us all very involved with her wedding plans. She's turning into quite the bridezilla, so I assume it's about that.

"Hey, are you okay?" I ask as he storms into the kitchen. I rub my tummy and get up off my seat, making my way over to see him.

"Blake? What's wrong?" Now I think that it might be me as well. All the guessing annoys me and is why I hate relationships. "Blake? Can you talk to me?" He takes bottled water out of the fridge, takes a sip and then places it back on the table.

"When you're ready to know, I will tell you." I shut my mouth, biting down on the inside of my cheek to stop me from answering back. He sits at the table, in the seat that I was occupying, and looks down at the paper.

"What the fuck is this?" he asks, glancing down at the circles that are drawn around numbers for apartment complexes.

"I can't live with you forever, Blake."

He shoots up out of his seat. "Yeah, you can. You're having my daughter Vicky, and I want to take care of you...*both.*"

That's bullshit and he knows it.

"Blake, the only reason you care is because I'm pregnant. Which is a good and bad thing? I have no doubt that you're going to make an amazing father, but I need to move on. I can't just live here with you." His face falls, and for the first time since I've known him, I think I see the pain in his eyes. He sits back down in his seat and looks up to me.

"I'm sorry that we never worked out. I wish I could get into the details of why this cannot happen right now, but I can't. I'm so fucking sorry because I fucking love you, Vicky. I love you so fucking much that I'm willing to let you go." I look into his eyes, shocked by his confession, and all I see is that same pain. I drop to the seat in front of him and place my hands on his cheeks.

"Talk to me, Blake. I've waited for you. I don't know what else I can do to make you see how much I want this, more than anything."

He smiles a slow smile at me. "One day I'll tell you. And when that day comes, Vicky? I will never, ever, let you go." I drop my hands in defeat, I can see in his eyes that his decision is set in stone.

I walk back to my room and begin packing up all my stuff, deciding that I'll stay in a hotel until I can find an apartment. There's no way I can stay here after that conversation.

And to think we were doing well.

He comes into my room, freshly showered with nothing but a loose pair of jeans on, his hair damp from his shower and his perfect, golden skin glistening from the water.

"What are you doing, Vicky?" he asks.

"I'm going to stay at a hotel. I can get an apartment quick, but I can't stay with you until then." I watch his jaw ticking as he walks over to me and snatches my bag.

"There's no fucking way I'm letting you stay at a hotel. You want to move into your own place? Fine. But you are staying here until then, and that *is* final."

I drop my arms in defeat. "What are we doing, Blake? You just told me you loved me. I'm so confused."

His face softens, and he makes his way over to me. "I thought that much was obvious. I wouldn't fucking be here if I didn't." I rest my head on his shoulders and he pulls me in under his arm, kissing me on the head.

I sigh. "I love you too, you know? I'm just frustrated that you can't tell me what's going on." His body stills, and he brings my face up to his, searching my eyes for something. I don't know what, but he's looking deep. He eventually blows out a ton of air and gets up from the bed.

"Stay here until you find a place, Vicky. I'll stay at the clubhouse." He then walks out of the room, picks up his keys and leaves with the final thing I hear being the deep rumble of his bike. A single tear drops from my eye, as I realize that we may never work.

I pull into my new apartment, and I love it. It's exactly what I need with two bedrooms and a modern layout, this will be perfect for when my little button comes along.

"Okay, that's everything. Let's go and set up her room!" Alaina says clapping her hands excitedly. I'm wearing my normal pregnancy get up—yoga pants and a T-shirt. My long hair in a loosely twisted bun, on the top of my head, with a pink bandana tied to the front.

Don't judge me. I'm eight months pregnant and moving house.

Luckily, the boys all helped us move.

"Do you know what's going on with Blake?" I ask Alaina. She looks to me with a small smile.

"He's trying to sort through some stuff right now, and *someone* is making threats. He wants this

Vicky, he really does, but right now I understand why he needs to keep you distant. In fact, I support it." I continue to pack all my clothes into the drawers, getting slightly frustrated with all the cryptic comments that I've had to put up with.

"That's all I have been hearing. The way I see it, he doesn't want me, and I can't—" I feel a tightening pull in my lower tummy, "Oh fuck." I clutch my bump and Alaina looks to me.

"What? Now? *Really,*" she exclaims, with excitement in her voice.

"Alaina, I can't go into labor now. I'm a month early!" I start to panic. That's when it feels as if a bucket of water has just shot down my legs. "Shit, my water just broke."

Alaina starts to run around the room, and if I weren't freaking out right now, it would make me laugh.

"Okay, where's your hospital bag? Tell me you've packed a hospital bag, Vicky!" She knows me too well, I am so disorganized and I leave things to the last minute, the complete opposite of what she is.

I put my hand up to my forehead. "Fuck. Okay, just throw in some body suits, her baby blankets, and baby wraps into the bag for now. I'll get Blake to come back and get the rest." She nods her head, and while she's doing that I begin to throw things into my bag. Once everything is packed, we walk downstairs and Alaina starts to make her way to her car.

"Um, Lain? No offense but my car is faster. There's no way I'm risking it in your little hatchback."

She rolls her eyes at me. "Hand them over, speed racer." I hand her my keys and get into the car. We hit the highway and Alaina are going well over the speed limit.

"I need to call Blake." I realize out loud. I pick up my phone and dial his number and he picks up quickly, like always. "Hey—" I cut him off. "Blake, I'm in labor. Lain is driving me to the hospital now."

"Shit! Okay, I'll meet you there."

After hanging up the phone, my contractions shoot in deeper. "Fuck Alaina, I don't know if I can make it there."

She glances over to me. "Oh, no you don't. Don't you fucking do this shit to me Vicky, we are three minutes away."

Pulling up to the hospital, Alaina jumps out and starts screaming that I need help because I'm about to push a baby out on this very road, making doctors and nurses rush over to me. They place me on a bed and just as they wheel me into my room, I begin to push.

"Vicky, you're going to have to slow down, hon. The next contraction you have, I want you to breathe through it, okay? It's going to hurt, but if you push, you'll end up with stitches from here to Africa. And trust me, you don't want those," the doctor says to me calmly. I nod my head and look up to the door, just as Blake comes crashing in. He comes straight to the side of my bed, kissing me on the forehead and taking my hand into his.

"I'm here, baby, and I got you. Let's meet our little princess."

After only a couple of pushes, and no pain relief, I'm now the proud mommy of a beautiful blonde haired, blue-eyed little girl. I know everyone says that their baby is the most beautiful little girl they've ever seen, but that's because they haven't seen little Pipper Carolee Rendon. Carolee is a mixture between my mother's and Blake's sister's nickname. When she found out that Blake and I were having a baby, she was so excited. Even though she hadn't then met me, we talk almost every week.

"I can't stop staring at her," I say to Blake.

"She's so beautiful and we made her," he replies, smiling up at me. When he looks at her, all I can see is one hundred percent love and it's such a beautiful thing to watch.

After two days of being in the hospital, we head home and settle back into my daily routine. Before I know it, it's been four months since Pipper arrived. I've caved in my house, hardly leaving, with Blake running around after us the whole time. He's all for his daughter and is completely in love with her. Anything between him and me is still non-existent. Sometimes I feel like he's seeing someone else. He looks after our daughter and me, but he hasn't made any advances since he got back from New Zealand, and we haven't spoken about our feelings for one another since I moved out of his house. It's currently a Friday night, and I get a text message from Alaina.

> Alaina: *Right mama bear, it's time for us to hit the town like old days.*

I laugh while picking up my phone.

> Me: *Oh yeah? And who is going to watch the cub?*

Pipper has had the nickname *'cub'* since her birth. Just as I get a reply, someone knocks on my door. Getting up to answer it, I see it's Phoebe.

"Hey Phoebs, what's up?" I greet her, letting her in. I haven't seen her in a few weeks, but I'm aware that she's been spending more time in Westbeach.

"I've come to babysit the little princess," she coos in a baby voice to Pipper.

"Alaina's idea?" I ask with raised eyebrows.

"Of course, when the queen speaks, you listen," she giggles while throwing her jacket onto the kitchen bench.

"All right then, I guess I should get ready," I say, making my way to my bedroom to find some clothes to wear.

An hour of shuffling through my wardrobe, Alaina finally finds something for me to wear.

"Alaina, I don't want to wear this, my body's not the same," I whine to her while looking at myself in the long mirror. "Vick, you had a baby and even then, your body is still banging." She's lying, my body will never be back to the way it was. My hips are wider and my ass is bigger, and my tummy isn't tight like it used to be.

"Thanks for the fake encouragement, Lain." She smiles up at me while we make our way out the door.

"I'm not lying, Miss Paranoid." We make our way out the front of my apartment, just as the taxi arrives.

"I can't believe I wore this," I say as we're getting in. I'm wearing a tight pastel purple baby doll dress, and black heels. My long dark brown hair is flowing in soft curls at the ends, and I'm wearing a bit more makeup than usual.

I put extra work in on my face, to make up for my fat ass.

We pull up to the club and I thought I would be excited, but all I feel is anxious. This is the first time I've been away from Pipper and I hate it.

"We stay till twelve and that's it?" I say to Alaina as we jump out of the car.

"Yes, I promise. Come on, mama bear. Let's drop that kitty down low." I pause our steps and laugh at her.

"Ew Lain, what have you been listening to? You've only been living away from me for a few months, and your music taste has already turned to shit." She hooks her arm around mine.

"Yeah, yeah. Let's go." I'm surprised Zane has let her out of his sight, this doesn't happen often. They have been trying for a baby, so they usually spend their free time having sex and I mean everywhere. We walk in and order some drinks. Luckily, I can actually drink now. I tried the breastfeeding thing, but my boobs are about as good as a dry nun.

We're back to our old antics, shooting down tequila when I feel a body brush up next to me. Looking up, I see that it's Ryder.

"Holy shit! What are you doing here?" I smile happily, pulling him into a hug. He's looking as good as ever in a white long-sleeved shirt rolled up to the elbows, showing off two arms that are completely covered in tattoos, and jeans with white Nikes.

Shit, he looks really good.

"I've been in the area for a few weeks." He smiles his bright smile and I blush. I look over to Alaina and see her fangirling, waiting for me to introduce her to him.

"This is Alaina...Alaina this is Ryder. No, I'm not going to tell you how I know him. And yes, Blake knows I know him," I say to her.

"Nice to meet you, Ryder. I'm a huge fan of Twisted Transistor!" She's fanning her face and embarrassing herself.

So after chatting for a while and saying goodbye to Ryder, I drag her out of there and toward the toilets. Once in the safety of the women's restrooms, she turns to me.

"Vicky, what the fuck? Oh my God, how do you know Ryder Oakley?" I look at her, wanting to slap the stupid out of her.

"I can't tell you, I'm sorry. But you will love me for doing it."

She laughs while splashing water on her face. "You know, I had to beg Blake to even let you come out tonight."

I walk up behind her and look at her in the mirror. "What do you mean? He was the one that decided I wasn't worth the fight, Alaina. Not me."

She drops her hands, turning to me. "I'm sorry, that was a dumb thing to say."

I wave my hands away. "Don't worry, it's forgotten. Let's go dance."

Ordering more shots, we shoot them up then move to the dance floor, where Brandon Beal's *'Twerk it like Miley'* comes blasting through the speakers. We start laughing, dropping it low and grinding up on each other in probably the most inappropriate of ways, but it's what we do. I turn my head around and see Blake sitting at the bar with the rest of the boys, them all watching us like hawks.

Stopping, I pull Alaina into me so I can whisper in her ear, "You invited them?" I ask.

She shakes her head before putting her face up to my ear. "I told them where we were going, but that's all. I swear." She throws her arms up. I roll my eyes and forget that they're there. Blake hasn't made a move on me since before he found out I was pregnant, he's not about to do it now. Which is a good thing, because the thought alone makes my skin burn with need. When the song finishes, it's followed closely by Papa Roach's *'Last Resort'* and I automatically look to Blake, knowing that he and I share the same love of good rock music.

He lifts his bottle to his lips, smirking around the rim before letting the drink drop down his throat. I keep dancing, not taking my eyes off him, watching as his eyes grow dark and needy. I haven't seen that look in months, and anytime I thought I had seen that look, I thought I'd imagined it. I turn my back on him as I begin to really dance, not being able to contain how much I'm turned on just by his stare. He could make me orgasm all over this floor with that look alone. I feel a body flush up against my back, so I spin around and meet his gasp.

"Oh, I exist?" I ask him innocently.

He wraps his arm around my back, pulling me into him. "You've always fucking existed, Vicky. But now, I don't give a fuck about anything else. I need to have you."

I laugh and stumble backward. "Tsk tsk biker man, your ship has sailed." I have no idea what I'm talking about. There's no way his ship has sailed. He pulls me back into him and pushes me up against a wall in the dark corner of the room.

Bringing his head down to my ear, he runs his perfect pouty lips around the edges.

"I don't believe you. I can feel you squirming under me as we speak." I start to breathe heavily. I'd be lying if I said that I don't feel disappointed in how I feel right now. I feel ready to open my legs up to this man in an instant, despite everything. *Whore.* One of his hands stays up against the wall beside my head, the other hand drops to cup my ass.

"Fuck, I love your body. I loved it then, but I love it even more now. This ass? Goddamn," he growls into my ear, setting alight a fire in between my legs. His legs push mine open until his crotch is pushing into mine. All I can feel is his huge bulge pushing up against me. I moan out a little at the contact making him bring his mouth over mine lightly while he slowly opens my mouth up with his tongue. He slides it over mine before it turns into a full-blown hungry kiss. My hands have flown up to wrap around his neck. He currently has me up against the wall with my legs wrapped around his waist.

"Blake?" He carries me through the crowd to an exit, pushing it open onto a dark back alley. I laugh while kissing him, as he pushes me up against the brick wall. I feel the roughness of the wall on my back, but I don't care. I want him and need him, *now.*

"Fuck, I've missed you, baby. I'm sorry. I'll explain it all to you tonight," he says, pausing what we're doing.

"Okay."

With that he moves his hands up my dress, moving my panties to the side and dipping his fingers into me massaging my g-spot. My eyes roll back in pleasure.

"You on the pill? A different pill?" he asks. I nod my head and he brings his hand up, pulling my dress down over my breasts, sucking each of them roughly. He runs his hand back down my dress and unzips his jeans, pulling his dick out and slamming it into me. I scream out at the contact that I have craved for so long. My need for this man is beyond normal, it's borderline obsession. He's pounding into me—hard. I feel myself tense up around his cock as my body begins to convulse from my orgasm. He pushes into me one last time before I feel his dick start twitching inside me.

"Holy fuck," I say while sliding down off the wall.

He hooks his finger under my chin, tilting my face up to his and kisses me sweetly on the lips. I smile and look over his shoulder just in time to see

Corrin, his ex-girlfriend, drawing a gun up and pointing it at him.

My need to protect the man that I love takes over me, and all sense leaves my body. I scream out, *"No!"* as I run in front of him, taking the bullet that she's fired right in my stomach. I fall to the ground, and my whole world turns black. The last thing I hear is Blake shouting, and a car tires screeching while taking off.

CHAPTER 19

BLAKE

I take Vicky under my arm as people start to crowd around us. For the first time in my life, I'm crying like a little bitch.

"Fuck baby, hang in there, please," I tell her frantically as I put pressure on her wound. I hear the ambulance pull up just as Alaina, Zane, and the rest of the boys round the corner.

"Oh my God, *Vicky!*" Alaina screams, running up to her while she lies over my legs. I wipe the tears from my eyes while still keeping pressure on the wound, smearing blood all over my face. This doesn't look good. I've seen these sorts of injuries before. Hell, I've caused these sorts of injuries before, and they never live, not in the stomach. Everyone's standing around me, and I look to Zane.

"It was *her*," I say, sneering the word *"her."* His eyes narrow and his jaw clenches before he nods his head. Once they have Vicky packed into the ambulance, with me right next to her, the rest of the boys follow us the whole way there.

Once we get there, a mob of doctors and nurses rush to her side and take her away. It all happens so fast, I blink and she's gone. I can't believe I fucking let this go on for so long, this is my fucking fault. I pull at my hair in frustration as I look around the waiting room. I see all the brothers here, as well as Alaina.

"I need to call her parents," I say, picking up my cell phone then I dial her parents' number. They're not too bad. Her mom liked me straight away, but her dad wasn't having any of it. Her dad picks up on the second ring.

"Jefferson, I'm sorry. Vicky's in the hospital and I think it's bad. You need to get here as soon as possible," I say to him. Another tear rolls down my cheek, out of frustration that it's all out of my control. I don't give a fuck if I'm crying. If anyone has a problem with it, I'll shoot them. This is my woman, my old lady, the mother of my daughter. This can't be happening, I need her.

"What? What do you mean?" he asks in a panicked tone.

"There was an incident tonight at a bar, and she's been shot. I'm so sorry."

After giving him all the details, I hang up my phone and put it back into my pocket. Ade comes up to me, with pain apparent in his eyes. It took him a while to warm up to Vicky, but after she had Pipper, his love for Pipper was so strong it carried on through to Vicky.

"I'm sorry, brother. But if anyone's able to pull through this it's Vicky," he says, throwing his arms around me. I tap his shoulders in appreciation as I sit back into my seat.

We wait for what feels like years when I see a doctor come out the doors. So I stand to make my way to him.

"Is she going to be okay?" He looks at me with sympathy in his eyes.

"I'm sorry, Mr. Rendon. At this stage all I can say is that we have the best possible team working on her. The bullet penetrated her stomach but missed all major organs. We're working the best we can to pull her through this," he answers. I stand there in shock.

"So, she is going to be okay? It missed all major organs, so she's going to live?" I ask with a little bit of hope.

"It is still early to say. For now, she's in a medically induced coma." Fuck! That doesn't sound good. I don't care if she's brain dead, I'll look after her until my last days. I will never leave her again.

"Can I see her?" I ask. He shakes his head.

"Not yet, you should go home and get some rest. Come back in the morning."

I should fucking punch him out for even thinking I'd leave her here alone. I walk back to the waiting room.

Alaina stands and makes her way to me. "What's happening?" I explain everything to her the best I can before I go and sit next to Zane.

"I know where she'll be and I'm going there now," I whisper to him.

He looks up to me. "I was thinking we bring her down through the system, and we can call Abby. Let's just lock the bitch up. There's CCTV footage all over that street, that's all the evidence we need. You don't want to go in blind, brother. It's what she wants."

I look over to him, my eyes dead. "It's Vicky this time, Zane. She got fucking shot! She took a fucking *bullet* for me. I need to kill Corrin."

He pushes back on his seat and bores holes into my head. He does this when he thinks I am not thinking clearly. "Think this through, Blake. It's not smart, this is a set-up. Don't do it. I can call Abby now. We have girls inside that will make her wish *every single day* that she was dead. Trust me, brother."

I think over his words, and they make sense. As much as I want to rip her fucking head off and feed it to pigs while pissing on her corpse, I like his idea better. She will suffer far longer than it would take for her to die.

"Done, make the call."

The next morning, all of Vicky's family are here. I thought that they would be swinging at me, especially Jacob, but they're not. They're just worried, waiting for news on her. I get up from the plastic seat and look around to see all my brothers asleep on their chairs, every single one of them, with Alaina curled up on Zane's lap. It makes me miss Vicky that much more. I should never have left her. I make my way over to Jefferson and Carol, giving them a hug, as well as Dominic and Jacob.

"Has the doc come back in?" I ask them all.

"Not yet, bro. What happened?" Dominic asks.

I explain what happened, and at the end I was ready for a few screams or fists thrown my way.

"That's Vicky, always trying to be a hero," her mother responds, with complete sadness in her voice.

"This was your fault?" Jacob asks with a straight face.

"She was my ex that shot the gun. So yeah, I guess it is." He shoots up off his seat, ready to hit me until Dominic pulls him back down.

"It's not his fault, Jake. It's Vicky and her fucking crazy ideas. Fuck," Dominic tells Jacob, making him sit back down in defeat. He brings his hands over his face in frustration, and I take that as my cue to leave.

"Blake? Who is watching Pipper?" Jefferson asks just as I turn to walk away.

"My sister has her at my place. You're more than welcome to go up there," I respond, before carrying on to sit by Zane.

"You call her?" I ask.

He nods his head. "Yeah, my man, it's all been done. As of this morning, she's in custody as we speak." He smiles at me and I smile back for the first time in three days. I *will* make sure she lives a miserable existence for the rest of her life, too.

"Mr. Rendon?" A young doctor comes out with her papers.

"Yeah?" I reply, walking straight up to her.

"Miss Abrahams is awake, and is asking for you," she says with a smile.

"Thank you." I give her a quick hug, before running into her room. When I get there, I see Vicky hooked up to wires and tubes. It makes my stomach ache. *Fuck! This is not fair.*

"Hey baby," I say to her, closing the door. "How are you feeling?" I ask, pulling up a chair so I can sit right next to her bed.

"I've had better days. How is Pipper?"

"She's at home still with Phoebe. Fuck, you scared me, baby." I kiss her hand as if my life depended on it. She smiles down at me briefly, but then her smile drops.

"And Corrin?"

"Locked up. We have a plan for her, don't worry about that," I say to her.

She smiles. "I'm sure you do."

"I don't want to live without you or Pipper, Vicky. I can't live without either of you."

She looks down at our joined hands. "Then don't. I've been waiting for you, Blake. You are my happily ever after."

Fuck, my heart feels like it stops just from her saying that. Fuck, this woman could kill me with her words.

"I love you, baby," I say to her, kissing her on the lips.

"I love you too, Blake."

The door opens and everyone walks in. I get up to tell them all to leave, but Vicky takes hold of my arm and shakes her head. Alaina straight away pulls over the covers and slides in next to her.

"Fuck Lain, be careful, please," I say to her, and she looks at me as if she's not bothered at all. She fits the queen role perfectly. Zane could not find a better partner. I pull my seat up to her head, letting her brothers in next to her.

"Vicky, don't you ever fucking do that shit again. I mean it." Jacob says, kissing her on the forehead.

"I'm sorry. Please don't be mad at me, or at Blake. It's not his fault, either," she says, and I see her looking directly at Jacob. She knows her brother *that* well. Jacob turns around and looks at me.

"You really do love him?" he asks Vicky. If he weren't her brother, I would fucking smash his face in just for questioning my position with her. Instead, I clench my fists.

"I love him, Jake, and he's the father to your niece. End of discussion."

Jacob looks to me and smiles. "All right then."

Still don't like the cocky fucker, don't care who he is.

I tap the seat and get up. "I'm going to call Phoebe to let her know what's happening, and to ask her to bring our girl down for a visit," I say to Vicky.

She smiles her beautiful smile at me. "That sounds perfect."

We're all still sitting in Vicky's room with her when Phoebe slams through the door with Pipper on her hip.

"Oh my God, thank God you're okay! Jesus Vicky, you scared the shit out of me."

I walk over to her and take hold of Pipper while doing the introductions to Vicky's family. I forgot that they hadn't met Phoebe. Alaina looks down to Vicky and then looks to Ade briefly.

"Should I call Kalie? Let her know what's happened?" I see Ade flinch at the mention of her name.

Vicky shakes her head. "No, there's no point now. She'll just flip out and drive down here. I'll let her know next time I see her."

CHAPTER 20

After everyone leaves, I sit next to Vicky with Pipper on my lap.

"You okay, baby?" I ask, taking her hand in mine.

"I'm okay, I'll be fine. Just promise me Blake, promise me you want this for the long run."

I look at her, squeezing her hand lightly. "Baby, I'm not going anywhere. You are it for me. I will spend the rest of my life making it up to you."

She smiles, then looks down to Pipper with her hands out. "Come here, princess."

I hand Pipper to her, and sit back and watch as Vicky plays with our daughter.

Our daughter.

My family unit was so small before I met Vicky. Now I feel as though it has expanded overnight.

My club and my sister will always be my family.

But these girls right here? They're my reason for living.

I need to marry this girl.

EPILOGUE

VICKY

Four Months Later

"Blake, she's walking along the furniture. Look!" I say to him as I point proudly at my little cub.

"Come here, my princess. Come to Daddy!" Blake says while kneeling on the ground, trying to entice her to walk to him.

"Blake, she's eight months, not one-year-old. She can't walk yet," I say, rolling my eyes. The door bursts open with Zane, Ade, Felix, Harvey, Chad, Ollie, Phoebe, and Alaina walking in.

"Come to your favorite uncle, pumpkin," Ade says, getting down next to her on the floor. Ade is an amazing uncle, as they all are.

I look over to Phoebe. "Are you all settled?" I ask her. Phoebe has just moved to Westbeach to continue her work from here. She decided she wanted to be closer to family, and her boss loves her that much that she decided Phoebe could fly in and fly out every week.

"I'm all settled, thank you for all the help," she says appreciatively to both Alaina and me.

"No problem, baby girl," Alaina replies as she lies down on the floor next to her goddaughter, beginning to play with her and Ade. I see Zane walk over to them possessively. I roll my eyes because some shit never changes.

"So, are we doing a barbecue at the clubhouse tonight?" I ask everyone.

"Yep, sure are. Should we head down there now and get started on prepping everything?" Alaina asks Phoebe and me. We both agree, and once we pack up a bag for Pipper, we make our way to the clubhouse leaving the men to sort out their club business.

Since Blake and I have been together, we decided to keep Sinsation. With Corrin in prison, it was automatically handed over to Blake. Who, as turns out, owns fifty-one percent of the club, as opposed to her forty-nine percent.

Pippa and I moved into Blake's house after I made him kid proof the entire thing, and while he was doing that, he decided to turn his whole backyard into the ultimate kid area complete with a playground and tree houses scattered all over the yard like little hobbit homes. I also run the books for Blake's construction company, which takes up a lot of my time. It's a huge company, with over fifty employees.

Yeah, full time.

Blake and I are doing really well. He tells me what I want to know regarding the club, but other than that, he tries his best to keep me out of all the bad shit. Because we have a daughter, he has more to lose. So he makes sure she's kept under wraps for the most part. But the club is my family, and right now, I could not be happier.

Once we arrive at the clubhouse, we unpack everything out of the trunk and make our way into the kitchen area. I start to make up the cheesecake while one of the prospects takes Pipper over to the playground to keep her busy. After we've done everything, all three of us make our way upstairs to get changed and ready for the night.

Coming back down, I take Pipper from Trevor and go sit by Blake.

"Here are my girls," he says, getting up and kissing us both—me on the lips and Pipper on the forehead. "I want you to meet someone." He points to a beautiful woman with dyed red hair and bright blue eyes.

Wow, she's really stunning.

"This is Abby, you've heard about her."

I nod my head and reach over to shake her hand. "Hi, it's nice to finally meet you," I say as I sit down next to Blake.

"Nice to meet you, too. And who's this beautiful girl?" she asks, holding her hands out to Pipper. I automatically hand her over, and I see Pipper loves her instantly. I smile at the sight in front of me. I look over to Phoebe, who's sitting right next to her brother and even though she's twenty-one, Blake will not let her out of his sight.

"Blake, let Phoebe go and socialize for fuck's sake," I whisper into his ear.

"No, fuck that. She attracts trouble, and there's a whole lot of trouble for her here," he says, taking a drink of his beer.

I mouth the word *"sorry"* to Phoebe. In her defense, I don't think the girl is into bikers. She's had a rough run as far as bikers go, and I wouldn't be surprised if she's gone off them altogether.

Her phone rings and a Twisted Transistor song starts blaring from it. I see her quickly shut it off, before looking over to see a questioning look from Blake.

"Oh for fuck's sake Blake, drop it," she says to him, before getting up to get herself another drink. I laugh around the rim of my glass at him.

Overbearing animal.

I look over to Zane and Alaina sitting opposite us on the picnic table, as they make out all over the place.

"Oh, come on. Really? Can't you two wait until you get home?" I sigh. Alaina laughs against Zane's mouth.

"We have an announcement to make." She smiles shyly at everyone. I start to get excited at the possibility of what this may mean. "We're pregnant," she bursts out, rubbing her tummy.

I jump up and clap excitedly. "Oh my gosh. This is so amazing!" I pull her into a hug and then let her go so everyone else can congratulate her, too. I know how long she and Zane have been trying and they're going to make incredible parents.

We're on our way home when Blake pulls up to the main beach and shuts off the truck.

"What's wrong?" I ask him, looking around at the dark beach. He opens his door and makes his way around to my side, pulling me out like a baby.

"Put this on," he says, pulling out the same lace blindfold from one of our first nights together, before picking me back up again.

I laugh. "Oh no way, homeboy. I'm a mama now. I can't roll like that anymore."

He pulls it over my eyes, squeezing my ass under his grasp. "There's no way in hell I'd let that shit go down again. Come on," he says to me, as he continues walking me down to the beach.

"Blake! Pipper can't stay in there on her own!" I yell at him, beginning to wonder what the hell he's thinking, leaving our baby in the truck on her own.

"She's not there alone, babe," he replies smoothly, making me peek under the blindfold to glance back to the truck over his shoulder. I see everyone standing there watching, with Alaina holding Pipper.

"Blake?" I ask him, confused. What just happened? How did we go from *family barbecue* to random late night walks on the beach? When he places me down, he walks behind me and removes my blindfold. When I look down, my hands fly up to my mouth in shock. "Oh my God!" I can feel tears prick at the side of my eyes. I'm standing in front of three giant heart shaped tea lights, all inside each other.

"It was the day after your party that I came down here to clear my head. That was that day, in this very spot that I realized I was in love with you. The big heart is mine, guarding yours and Pipper's, who are in the middle. I will always protect you two. You are both my world, and I want to spend the rest of my fucking life showing you that. You're my queen, Vicky. You've owned my heart since day one." He smirks and drops to one knee. "Will you marry me, baby?"

At this point, tears are streaming down my face. I nod my head up and down. "Yes. Yes!"

He places the ring on my finger and grabs onto the back of my legs, swinging my body over his shoulder, and runs me into the warm water.

"Blake!" I pout at him once I've come up for air.

"Oh, don't pout, baby." He runs his thumb over my bottom lip, before kissing me gently.

I look into his eyes, his hair is all wet and messy.

This sexy man is going to be my husband.

And with that, I can finally be his happily ever after.

THE END

Next by Author Amo Jones

Tainted Love

Sinful Souls MC Book Three

Kalie and Ade's Story

Kalie-Rose is that girl.
She's that girl who calmed the storm within Ade Nixon.
She attained the unattainable.
She silenced his demons with her innocence.

Ade Nixon is the Vice President of Sinful Souls MC. His Hulk-sized body covered in tattoos and piercings—along with his don't give a fuck attitude—screams, *'I'll suffocate you in your sleep.'* And he would.

Kalie-Rose is a popular dancer living in Hollywood Hills, she dances for some of Hollywood's elite. After giving Ade her virginity on a silver platter two years ago, a wedding brings them back together. Even if only for a short amount of time.

*This book contains upsetting content, which may set of triggers.

Metallica - “The Unforgiven”

Avenged Sevenfold - “Hail to the King”

Papa Roach - “Last Resort”

Brandon Beal - “Twerk it like Miley”

Metallica - “Fade to Black”

Thank you for reading Intricate Love,
I hope you enjoyed reading it as much as I enjoyed writing it. Book Three—Tainted Love—in the Sinful Souls MC series is now available for purchase.

Stay tuned for my new series "Westbeach" which is coming soon, kicking off with Ryder and Phoebe's story - "Losing Traction."

Thank you again to all my beautiful readers, thank you for all your kind words and encouragement.

You all inspire me to keep going—Thank you.

Goodreads

Add these books to your TBR list.

Perilous Love – Sinful Souls MC Series Book One

Intricate Love – Sinful Souls MC Series Book Two

Tainted Love – Sinful Souls MC Series Book Three

Losing Traction – Westbeach Series Book One

One Hundred and Thirty-Six Scars – The Devil's Own Book One

Website

http://www.amojonesauthor.com/

Twitter

https://twitter.com/authorAmojones

Email

amojonesauthor@yahoo.com

Facebook

https://www.facebook.com/amojonesauthor?ref=hl

Goodreads

https://www.goodreads.com/author/show/14047384.Amo_Jones

Instagram

https://instagram.com/authoramojones/

A little bit about me. I am the mama bear to four little kiddos, two girls, and two boys. I'm also a wife-to-be to my partner of ten years. We were high school sweethearts, without the high school. My little (big) family are my rock, and I'm so lucky to have them with me through it all.

I am from New Zealand! Born and raised in a small town called Rotorua. It's a beautiful city, just smells a little. I'm currently living in Australia on the Whitsunday Coast (Great Barrier Reef) where we hope to settle down for a long time. I love the beach, and margaritas, and wine. Don't forget the wine. Chinese food is the best food.

One day I hope to travel the world, preferably the US, because I'm obsessed with it. I would travel now, but my bank account is like..."Dude, no." So I've put that in the goal bucket.

I love all my beautiful readers, you have kept me going. You're my inspiration to keep writing, with all your kind words and reviews. You are all amazing, and I write for you.

That's enough yappin' from me. See you all in Wonderland. x

Namaste.

Printed in Great Britain
by Amazon

46751804R00149